THE DEAD
& THE DYING
STAY DEAD BOOK TWO

STEVE WANDS

ISBN: 0615803199
ISBN-13: 978-0615803197

DEDICATION

Dedicated to Drew, Eddie, Joe, Nonni, and Big Richie.

CONTENTS

Acknowledgments   ix

Author's Note   xi

Prologue   1

1 Road warriors   5

2 Barbie the Zombie Killer   11

3 All messed up   16

4 Wheels   18

5 We've got company   24

6 Scavengers   28

7 Loose end   33

8 Expect delays   38

9 When Sarah met Jim   43

10 Special occasion   48

11 Only in dreams   53

12 Impulses   58

13 Left behind   64

14 Mashed brains   69

15 Old man moment   72

16 Off-Roading   77

17 Raiders   80

18 Hold on   83

19	Free lunch	87
20	Big bad wolf	90
21	Nothing but darkness	93
22	Something wicked	96
23	Back on course	99
24	Despair	102
25	Are we there yet?	105
26	Heart of the matter	109
27	Just the wind	112
28	Low on options	117
29	Nancy Nedermeyer	121
30	End of the road	124
31	Starting to pile up	128
32	Like a graveyard	131
33	Yard work is hard work	134
34	The Bridge	137
35	Stockpiling	140
36	Through the wreckage	144
37	Endurance test	148
38	The Cell	152
39	Don't look in the car	154
40	A familiar Odor	157

41   Now or never   160

42   Suicide Run   164

43   Teeth and glass   168

44   Skin mask   171

45   Goodbye, New Jersey   174

46   That sad smile   177

47   It's always crowded   180

48   The Protean   184

49   Captain Chuck   187

50   Farewell   191

51   Living dead   194

52   A dead city by the sea   197

53   Just one more day   201

54   Fading light   205

55   Wishful Thinking   208

56   Vengeance on the wind   211

     Epilogue   214

ACKNOWLEDGMENTS

To my family and friends for your support.
To my wife—for everything. To my son—for being awesome. To Adam
Staffaroni for coming on board as editor. To my first readers, Keith Latch,
Darryl L. Pierce, and Desmond Reddick. Thank you all.

AUTHOR'S NOTE

This novel takes place in a fictionalized version of our world. We spend a lot of time in New Jersey and up the eastern coastline with a quick glimpse at West Virginia but they are not quite the states as you know them. Any resemblance to actual incidents, or to any person living or dead, is purely coincidental.

The most beautiful thing we can experience is the mysterious. It is the source of all true art and all science. He to whom this emotion is a stranger, who can no longer pause to wonder and stand rapt in awe, is as good as dead: His eyes are closed.

—Albert Einstein

PROLOGUE

West Virginia.
Mount Weather Special Facility.

Rachel Lucas and Doctor Gregory Tran put in a request to work together. They had to justify the request with their superiors and upon furnishing their findings they had gotten what they wanted. With a catch, of course.

A young soldier sat restrained on the examination table usually reserved for the dead. He was a blond haired kid from Texas barely old enough to drink. He was heavily sedated but his eyes were penetrating, and nothing but terror and oblivion could be seen in them. It was gut wrenching just to look at him.

After hearing what the catch was Rachel tried everything she could to stop it from happening, but failed. When she was given the choice to take the soldier's place she decided to keep her own. As a result she felt responsible for the young man's predicament. She tried to tell herself he'd end up dead anyway, but it still hurt.

The kid soldier was hooked up to a mechanical respirator in the hopes that once given a lethal injection his brain would still be getting oxygen. In theory it would present Rachel and Tran with the best possible specimen in which to continue their research. They also had a medical infusion pump and a dialysis machine in the corner of the room should they decide to use them.

Several guards stood outside of the room accompanied by the

Deputy Secretary of Defense, William T. Pymn II, who nodded for Tran to carry out the lethal injection. Tran grimly nodded back. He too didn't want to sacrifice a soldier of all people, but figured it was better than the alternative.

He administered the injection and the young man tried to squirm but was too heavily restrained to move. Tran and Rachel watched the monitors as the young man died before them. His heart stopped first and then all brain activity ceased. The mechanical respirator kept him breathing as planned.

Moments later his eyes opened even though clinically he was dead. He had no pulse, no heartbeat, and brain activity that reflected it was dying. Yet he could speak.

"Brains," the thing muttered. "Flesh," as his jaw moved and his eyes flitted around the room.

"What is your name?" Tran asked.

"Death."

"Are you Private Richard Barret?"

"Deatthhh."

Rachel asked, "Is Richard in there?"

"Yesss."

"Can we speak to him?"

"Hee sssscreammsss."

"Is he in pain?"

"Yesss."

"Is death painful?" Asked Tran.

"Yesssssss."

"I think his speech is starting to digress."

"Why are the dead coming back to life?"

"Flessshh."

"Answer the question. Why are the dead coming back to life?"

"Tiiiime…ffforrrrr theeee…unnnwiindinnngggggg."

"What is that?"

"Yyyyoourrrr…ffffleesshhhh—

"Hold it together!"

"What is the unwinding?"

"Yyyoourrrr…ennnnd…yrrrrrrrrgggggnnnuhhhh."

"I can feel it. Whatever we were talking with is gone."

Tran nodded in agreement. He could feel it too. His hands were like ice, but the back of his neck was wet with sweat.

He pulled a surgical gag from a cabinet and put it in the dead Private's mouth.

"What the fuck did I just hear?" The Deputy Secretary of Defense, William T. Pymn II, asked as he stormed into the room.

"It would appear," Tran started, but couldn't believe what was about to come out of his mouth, "that we just spoke with the entity of Death."

"This is absurd. We just put a good man to death, and his drug-addled last words are supposed to be those of the boogeyman? I should put a bullet in both of your heads right now."

"With all due respect, sir, you can't ignore what just happened. You don't believe it, that's fine, but I'll put my life on the line here and say that if we did this experiment again, it would yield the same results."

"You put your life on the line the second you opened your mouth, Tran, and if you open it again I'll strap you down to that table myself and let this little lady over here experiment on you."

Tran new better than to push any further, so he stood there and took the verbal affront as if he were a dog being scolded for snatching bread off the table.

"Ms. Lucas, would you put your life on the line as well?"

"Yes, sir, I would."

"Fine. I'll clear you to do it again, but I'm not wasting another man on so little. I thought we would have seen something more definitive than this. Report to me first thing tomorrow and I'll figure out another way of getting you fresh bodies."

"Yes, sir."

The Deputy Secretary of Defense turned and left the room as if he had somewhere better to be and his armed guards left with him, aside from the one stationed at the outside of the room.

Rachel waited till Pymn was out of sight before she took a deep breath and said, "Well, that was interesting."

"Yes. Nothing like staring the devil in the face and convincing yourself it's a Halloween mask."

"Maybe Pymn doesn't believe in things like Death as an entity."

"Regardless of your belief system, the dead are alive and walking. I don't know about you, but for me, that changes the way I look at everything—even something as archaic as religion, or as existential as death."

"What do you think he'll do?"

"I know what I would do. Are you familiar with the area, Ms. Lucas?"

"Not really."

"West Virginia Penitentiary."

"Prisoners? So much for cruel and unusual punishment."

"I don't think the rules of yesterday matter much anymore."

"I suppose not, and I suppose its better to use the condemned than it is to use our own soldiers."

"Of course, I'm just taking a guess here."

"Well, I'll bet a hundred bucks you're right."

"If only I were a gambling man."

"Not like money has any value now."

The Deputy Secretary of Defense, William T. Pymn II, went right to work on solving the problem of finding non-military test subjects. Three days after the world went to hell Pymn has suggested using prisoners to assist military units on the ground war. He had little political backing for the proposition and was unable to gain any traction. By the time he was given the green light he was already sequestered away to the Mount Weather Special Facility and swept up in the day-to-day of the facility.

He was not entirely convinced that the voice from the dead soldier was Death itself, but the prospect of it was chilling to say the least, though Pymn would never show it. Even if it ended up being nothing, at least it would give him the opportunity to acquire the prison—if it was still operating—either by force or cooperation.

He had thought on it a great deal. He had already gone so far as to approach some of his own men with the prospect of commanding such a unit, and many of them could see the upside of commanding a unit of prisoners—especially prisoners on death row or serving life. It didn't matter if you sent a man like that to his death, because as far as society was concerned they were better off that way.

He decided it was time to make some calls and send a unit to the West Virginia Penitentiary.

1 ROAD WARRIORS

The mostly leafless Oak trees and cold grey skies made the world seem all the more dead on its feet. The sun hung in the air, but its heat could not be felt—it was a chilly day and bitterly so. The wind howled through the trees, shaking loose whatever resilient leaves still hung on by a thread. On one tree, a small spindly Black Maple that looked almost sickly, a beautiful red and orange Maple leaf hung on longer than all the others. Its stem holding strong against the blustering breeze while its brethren had given up and fallen to the ground, only to dry up and be crunched underfoot of an animal and the dead things it scurried from.

An abandoned Labrador with a black collar and matching leash erratically ran through the woods away from the dead things. She would stop and bark at them, attempting to scare them off, but then she would run away again—as if she knew they would not scare. Following the dog were several deaders as lifeless as the leaves under their feet. The dog looked ragged and wafer-thin. Its hair was beginning to fall out and like the leaves on the trees its life wasn't long for this world.

The chocolate Labrador labored heavily to suck in enough oxygen to keep its legs pumping. Up ahead was a road, she just had to push herself a little harder to get up the hill, and then maybe she could loose them. She didn't let up and her legs carried her up the small hill and to the edge of the road where she didn't even bother to stop and look. She ran straight across, hooked to the right, and then disappeared into the woods on the other side.

"Whoa! Did you guys see that? It was a dog. Just ran across the road," Dawn said.

Dawn had been aching for a cigarette. She had only a few left and couldn't wait till they stopped so she could have one. When she used to work late nights at the diner she'd be outside smoking as often as possible. When she couldn't make it to work on account of the living dead, smoking and surviving was all she had left.

Jon-Jon pointed to the woods and struggling to get to the street were the several deaders that had been chasing the dog, "Looks like those fuckers over there were chasing it."

"Ugh. You think they're going after animals now, too?" Dawn asked, thinking one of the deaders looked like one of the younger dishwashers.

"I don't see why not, but maybe they were just chasing the noise? Maybe their eyeballs are all gone? Who the fuck knows," Jon said, returning his attention to the road.

Dawn stared at the dead things in disgust and anger. They raised their arms toward the van. Whether or not their eyeballs were working they knew that something edible was nearby. Dawn flipped them the bird and her look of anger shifted into a look of pure hatred.

Jon-Jon turned the radio on again.

"It's just going to be the same thing," Dawn protested.

"Well, I like the way it sounds—fella has a nice deep voice."

… those areas we will reinstate the Emergency Transportation System to aid survivors in getting to those locations.

We will continue repeating this Emergency Alert System broadcast until we have new information.

This is an Emergency Alert System broadcast originating from the Mount Weather Special Facility in West Virginia.

There is a worldwide phenomenon occurring where clinically dead humans are reanimating and attacking living humans in an attempt to eat living flesh. Early attempts at dispatching the reanimated hostiles, destroying the brain, seemed effective. However, new evidence suggests we now warn that this is insufficient. Specimens assumed dead continue to reanimate. There is no consistent timeframe for which a hostile will reanimate. The only permanent way of dispatching the hostiles is by incineration, or the use of a chemical agent to dissolve the remains.

It is also safest to stay off the roads and out of heavily populated areas. If you have found a safe haven it is recommended you remain there. Specially equipped units of the military are in the process of reclaiming key strategic areas around the nation. Once we are able to reclaim those areas we will reinstate the Emergency Transportation System to aid survivors in getting to those locations.

We will continue repeating this Emergency Alert System broadcast until we have new information.

"Looks like we got an accident over here."

"Can we get through?" Eddie asked from behind them.

"Looks like no problem. I don't see any deaders either."

Jon-Jon cautiously drove up to the accident. A small sedan was wrecked by a larger SUV. The SUV had smashed in the side of the car and most of its front. A third car looked to have been unable to break in time and rear-ended the SUV. There were no bodies in the cars, only a trail of old blood that looked like dirt coming from the smaller sedan.

Eddie had moved forward from the back and crouched down in front to peer out the windshield, "Guess if there were any they're long gone now."

Dawn turned to him, "Looks that way."

Dawn looked worn out. Her cheeks had sunken in over the course of the few days that they had come to know each other. They hadn't much food left, and the lack of sleep and constant levels of elevated stress weren't helping much. Dawn could probably say the same thing for anyone in the van or in the two vehicles behind them. Eddie himself, who had become somewhat of a leader of the group, looked wild and ragged. His hair was all over the place, his eyebrows looked crazy and his beard was growing bigger by the day—and unevenly.

The van itself smelled like a gym locker room—and that was with the windows down.

Chuck, who missed his home in sunny Florida, fell asleep, though every time the van hit a bump his head bounced off the window and he woke for a moment, only to fall back to sleep again. Sitting next to him was Janice—Eddie and Joseph's mother—and though she wasn't sleeping she looked catatonic and a breath away from death. Losing her husband and two younger children to the living dead seemed to take all but a sliver of life from her. Chung-Hee sat on the floor and tried to stretch. His legs had become cramped and he thought it was because he wasn't drinking enough water, and he was right. When he was holed-up at Mal-Mart he hadn't worried about that, there was plenty to be had.

Eddie left the front of the van to sit back at his brother's side. Joseph, who was physically larger, and stronger than his older brother, looked just as tired as everyone else, but maybe his age allowed him to deal with it better. His disposition seemed better every day, as did his resolve. He was pulling a strength from some place unseen whilst just about everyone else was losing it. Next to him was Frankie, who had been one of Eddie's closest friends since middle school, and Frankie just looked sucked dry of color and emotion. He had that two-thousand-yard stare that veterans would often talk about; the look from Thomas Lea's painting of the same name, the one with the soldier staring right at you with his eyes so wide and his mouth only slightly agape.

Driving cautiously behind them was Abdul-Ba'ith whose face never seemed to change even in the slightest manor. He looked dead serious and tight-lipped with an unmoving pair of bushy eyebrows. He'd joined up with the convoy after a chance meeting at a gas station, which they left in flames. He drove with both hands on the wheel and though he must've been just as tired as the others he made a point to sit up straight and stay alert.

To his right was Carrie, who'd been hiding out at the gas station with Abdul Ba'ith and several others days ago, the ever anxious and always annoying chubby dyke who turned out not to be a dyke at all. She chewed on her knuckles and fingernails as if they were snacks and even caused a few of them to bleed.

Alexis in the backseat had fallen asleep with the children. She was a young woman who'd dreamed of being a mother one day, like so many others, and found herself with a nightmare version of that dream. The children had fallen asleep on the drive, and seeing no reason not too Alexis closed her eyes and joined them. Leela, Chris, Nick, Stacey, and Yussef all slept together with crisscrossing limbs that would shift every few minutes to try to get comfortable. Some had parents that were lost along the way, while others were saved during the convoy's travels.

Holding the back of the line was Scott and Judy, a quirky married couple that owned and operated their own Funeral Home. They were used to dealing with dead people on a daily basis, but the living dead had proven to be a whole different beast altogether. They were talking about the good times: vacations, parties, and their honeymoon. Scott usually wasn't much for taking trips down memory lane, but Judy loved it and it put a smile on her face and if that's what it took for Scott to see that smile then that's what he'd do. It was that smile of hers that kept him going.

"You think we're doing the right thing?"

"I don't know babe. Going North seems like a good move. The broadcast could be a false hope. We could get down there and find ourselves in a worse situation. Just think of how many people might be trying to get there."

She thought about that for a moment...

What if everyone who'd heard the broadcast decided to try and get to West Virginia? It would just be chaos. She could picture the streets already clogged with abandoned vehicles and other obstacles, and now to picture them with other survivors trying to get to a safe haven. It would be just as bad as the first few days. The fights, the violence, only now it was harder to get anywhere because you had to go through all of the ruin that remained from those early days, and the dead. The first days were hard because of the living, now it was the living dead that complicated matters.

Scott turned the volume up on the broadcast.

--tent timeframe for which a hostile will reanimate. The only permanent way of dispatching the hostiles is by incineration, or the use of a chemical agent to dissolve the remains.

It is also safest to stay off the roads and out of heavily populated areas. If you have found a safe haven it is recommended you remain there. Specially equipped units of the military are in the process of reclaiming key strategic areas around the nation. Once we are able to reclaim those areas we will reinstate the Emergency Transportation System to aid survivors in getting to those locations.

We will continue repeating—

Then he abruptly turned it off. He was already sick of hearing it.

***

The blood from the dead man's body emptied onto the cold tile floor. It was dark, almost muddy, and oozed like old motor oil from a lawnmower that should've been changed seasons ago. Danni couldn't help but stare at it. Aside from the walls, and floor it was the next best thing to focus on. Everything else was too gruesome—too maddening—and just too damn hopeless to look at let alone think about.

Sherriff Bruce Davis, the man who was going to save New Haven by walling off the town, sat with his back against the wall and his eyes staring up at the ceiling. Though the town was probably dead, he was still thinking of a way out. He refused to resign himself to a fate so ironic—if only the dead grasping between the bars were people he himself had put away it would be almost poetic. Davis didn't like poetry, irony, and he sure as shit didn't like the idea of wasting away in a holding cell surrounded by the dead.

Clem on the other hand, looked ready for death. He had that far away look of resignation that Davis so adamantly refused to wear. It was written in his face. His eyes said 'take me now', and so did the crease in his forehead. He longed to be with his wife again. Back at their apartment before all this had happened. Before he found Danni on his rooftop. Before they tried to leave. Before he lost Lorraine. He stared at the dead things, all those thoughts running through his mind, looking at them with sad eyes and the taste of empathy in the back of his throat.

Topher, whom Davis and his men rescued while investigating the power station, was a sniveling mess. He kept murmuring to himself and wiping the tears from his eyes. He sat against the wall with his legs pulled in tight. He wanted to roll up into a ball and disappear. Sitting next to him, and just growing aggravated by Topher, was Keith. His face was stone and his knuckles were white. He wanted to beat Topher to death. All he could think about was Jones, his dead brother in blue, and knew that he was somewhere in the room beyond the bars and trying to get inside to eat him like all the other dead things were. The thought of it pissed him off big time.

"What the fuck are we going to do Bruce?"

"We're not going to do anything. We're going to sit and wait…and see what happens, unless you got a better idea."

Keith did not, and that pissed him off more.

Outside the cell they couldn't see anything other than the dead. They blocked out most of the light and filled the room with a putrid scent the likes of which none of them had ever smelled.

2 BARBIE THE ZOMBIE KILLER

Walter and Jeff Caulfield, father and son, huddled by the window once more to watch as the dead staggered about. New Haven had become infested with the dead. Walter wanted to know his enemy, so he tried to study them, but studying them hadn't really given him any greater understanding of the creatures or any alleviation of the concerns he and his family had. Some would walk toward the house while others would walk in other directions. Some followed others and there seemed to be no rhyme or reason behind any of it. It left them both as confounded as ever.

"Should we go back out?"

"No, not yet. I'm not as young as you are Jeffy-boy. Takes me a bit longer to get my wind back."

Jeff couldn't help but smile at the words Jeffy-boy. He couldn't recall the last time his father called him that. It had to be sometime in high school—maybe when Walter was teaching him how to drive around the parking lot. Yes, that seemed right. Walter handed him over the keys and the pimple-faced Jeff with three proud whiskers on his chin took them with vigor, and his father said, "Guess I can't be calling you Jeffy-boy anymore, huh?" And that was it. Jeffy-boy turned into Jeff—all grown up in the blink of an eye.

They could hear Laura, Walter's wife, Barbara, his daughter, and Maria, Jeff's wife playing with the children in the basement. The sound was soft and barely audible upstairs, but the house was otherwise quiet. Their laughter and giggles seemed an odd contrast to what Walter and Jeff were seeing outside the windows, but a very pleasing one. It was the sounds of hope and love. The sounds any man really needs to hear to get off his ass and make a move for the future. Walter used Jeff's shoulder to push himself up, and as his knees cricked and creaked and the pain burned deep in his back, he used the sounds of his grandchildren at play to push it away.

Jeff looked at his father approvingly and as Walter looked back at him all he could see was his little Jeffy-boy looking back. The skin around his eyes looked older, but the eyes themselves belonged to the little boy Walter would always see in them.

"Ready old-timer?"

"Nope. You?"

"I've been ready to fight zombies since I was Tommy's age."

"Heh. I guess all that garbage you used to watch might finally be worth a damn."

"Let's go find out."

They went into the half-finished basement where everyone was playing. Laura turned instinctively and without a word knew they were going back outside. Her and Walter looked at each other. She nodded in that disapproving way that made Walter smile and lift his eyebrow up a notch, suggesting he knew better, but he just couldn't help himself.

Jeff and Maria hadn't quite developed the fluid and succinct nuance of expression to convey their feelings, so Maria just looked at Jeff with incredulous and accusing eyes. Then she said, "Are you kidding? You're both going back out there?"

Jeff gave her a mean look, shifting his eyes to the kids, "We're...just going to check things out is all. Relax, we'll be right back, okay?"

"Whatever."

"I'm coming too," Barbara said.

"What? Why?"

"Why not dad? Is this boy stuff?"

"Boy stuff? Ha. Come on, now, it's not like that. The kids need you in here. Have fun. Trust me, you're better off."

"Well, if you're just going to check things out, then I'll be fine, right?"

Jeff smiled at her, but it wasn't a nice smile. It was the I'm-going-to-kick-your-ass-later smile. "She's right dad, why not? Come on, Barbie."

"You know I hate that."

Walter turned around shaking his head. The kids went back to playing. Tommy looked after his father, wanting to go with him and Laura tried to pull his attention back.

"Barbie The Zombie Killer," Jeff said as they went up the stairs.

"Don't be a dick. Can you bait your own hook yet, or does Maria have to do that for now?"

"Funny."

They walked toward the front door. The hall had a coatrack and bench in it with a small rug atop the hardwood floor. It wasn't a big space but it essentially served them as a mudroom. Hanging on the coatrack were a long raincoat and a slick jacket that Walter had used to go fishing with for years. It was supposed to be black, but it looked like seaweed green.

Jeff opened the closet door across from the bench at rummaged around a moment. He eventually pulled out an old track jacket with a hood and tossed it at his sister.

"There's a set of gloves in there," he pointed, "but I think you're on your own for boots."

"My sneakers are fine. I don't plan on getting myself all dirty. That's not very lady like."

"That's my girl," said Walter.

They opened the door and Walter grabbed the bloody shovel he left against the siding. Jeff took a step to the side and grabbed a baseball bat. He handed it to his little sister and she took it, finally showing a touch of fear on her face. Jeff grabbed the spade shovel that was next to Walter's and they descended the steps.

The dead things were walking around, seemingly without direction or purpose. One noticed them, and then another, before they reached the first deader several had turned their attention and their bodies towards them. Moving, slowly, at the warm flesh that in turn was moving towards them.

"Maybe I should've stayed inside."

"Next time, sweetheart, take my advice…for once, please."

"They get scarier up close."

"What do you mean?"

"Just look in their eyes. There's nothing there. It's like they're hollow."

"I don't think I want to get that close."

"Then stand back," Walter said, as he approached the first deader in proximity.

Walter jabbed the dead thing just under the chin, but not quite in the throat. It moved back and tripped on its own feet. They were easily thrown off balance and to the ground but surprisingly quick to get back up. Once the dead thing hit the ground Walter stood on its chest and brought the shovel down violently into its face, smashing through the bridge of its nose and crushing in its orbital sockets. Walter pulled the shovel out and jabbed it two more times in quick succession before taking his foot off the dead things chest and looking at where the others were.

"Look, dad, it's twitching."

"Yeah, I've been noticing that. Saw one earlier that was pumping its hand into a fist, like it was trying to grab the air."

"It's creepy as hell," Jeff noted.

"Sure is. All the more reason we need to keep watching them. Studying them. We need to know our enemy as best as possible."

"Watch out, dad, I'll take this one."

Jeff swung his spade shovel like a sword, cracking a dead man who had to be about the same age as he. The impact was strong and sent the man to the ground. The blow must have dislocated the man's jaw because it looked crooked and out of place. Jeff took the corner of the shovels head and slammed it into the deader's temple—cracking open its skull on the first shot. Then he stood on the corner of the shovel and pushed it in as if he were digging a hole. He pulled it out and did it again. The second assault seemed to nullify the dead thing.

Barbara stepped closer to it and after seeing its head she vomited.

"It's okay sweetheart. Jeff and I both puked earlier. No shame in it. Let's call it a night and head back in okay?"

"No. No, it's okay. I'm okay. I…I want to hit one."

Walter was a bit taken aback. Barbara always felt she had to prove herself to her father. If Jeff could do something then she had to make sure she was just as capable. No matter how many times Walter told her she had nothing to prove he might as well have been talking to himself, or a wall. A wall, he figured, might have listened before his daughter.

Barbara started moving toward one of them. She held the baseball bat down low, moving it around. She was getting comfortable with its weight, and as she moved closer to the dead thing she could see what Jeff was talking about. She could see the emptiness in its eyes. The lack of expression on its face. It really was just a dead thing. The only thing human about it was its appearance.

She swung, and hit it in the head. It moved backward, stumbling, but didn't fall. She swung again, this time putting her weight into it and knocked it over. She let out a small cry of disgust. What was she doing, she thought. She started to heave, and turned away with tear-filled eyes, "I can't do it. I can't look at it anymore."

Jeff stepped in and bashed its head in. Walter wrapped his arm around his daughter and led her back home. Jeff was quickly behind them.

"That's enough for now."

"I'm sorry, daddy, I couldn't—

"Shh, don't worry sweetheart. It's okay. I'm happy you couldn't. I wish I couldn't."

"So much for Barbie The Zombie Killer."

"You're such an asshole!"

"Oh come on."

"Can it. I swear the two of you will never grow up."

3 ALL MESSED UP

He should've been dead days ago, if not from loss of blood then surely by dehydration, but death just wasn't taking. He was in and out of consciousness; the only constant was the pain he felt throughout his body. He thought he had lost his mind. Surely he was dying, yet days had passed, or so he thought. He couldn't say with any certainty. He began to hear voices and feel out of his body at times. Moments passed when he felt as if something were in him, not in a physical way, more like he was of two minds, but the other mind wasn't his.

Then he felt it.

Ben sat up, no longer clutching the wound at his stomach.

"What are you?"

He received no answer, but felt an understanding ripple across his mind and with that he stood up. Ben stood tall and felt great, all things considered. He could feel a cold sensation throughout his body. He could also tell that he was dead. He didn't know how he knew, but he knew. He checked for a pulse anyway, and not surprisingly, didn't find one. He stuck his finger in the maggot filled bullet hole in his gut, swirling it around. He felt no pain, and when he pulled his finger out it was covered in a dark brown blood that had been coagulated for days. Again, he felt a ripple of understanding surge through him.

"Damn, how the hell do you even know what I was going to ask?"

Ben spun around looking for something, or maybe someone, but he saw nothing. The sky held no answers for him, so he turned to look down at the ground, and in a way an answer was there. The dead had left. He could feel the understanding wash over him. He was one of them. He wasn't hungry for flesh, but he wanted death. He still had all his senses, his ability to speak and think. Clinically he knew he was dead—he could feel it. He still didn't really understand why, and whatever force, or entity, or whatever was in his mind didn't have much of an answer. A few ripples surged through him, but nothing with the definitive quality as the ones before it. Ben got the impression that there was no real reason. It was part curiosity, part indifference, and oddly part entertainment. Whatever darkness was inside Ben wanted him to do what he'd always loved to do, and that was, quite simply, to kill.

Ben climbed down from the roof. He wanted to clean himself up and get a good look at himself in the mirror.

The school was empty, as were the grounds nearby. From what Ben could tell—and now feel, somehow—there were no deaders around. He made his way to the bathroom, turned the faucet on and cleaned his face and hands of all the dried blood and dirt that had become a second skin to him. He plucked the maggots off his body and flicked them into the sink. Then he patted his hair down and tried to comb it with his hands. He noticed a small clump came out as he wet it down and tried to fan it out. Flicking the clump of hair into the sink he looked at himself in the mirror angrily. The reflection showed his waning pallor and sunken eyes. Even his skin felt and looked to have a rougher quality too it.

"Even dead, I ain't too bad looking," Ben said, leaving the room.

Walking down the street Ben could feel where the blood had pooled in his body while he was dying. He could feel the coagulated blood sticking like honey to his innards as gravity pulled it down. His legs grew heavy and started to swell, but still he thought he felt great. The sun was warm, heating his cold flesh as he walked to the truck. He reached inside his pocket and found he still had the keys on him. He started the truck and sat in it for a moment unsure of where to go. His body filled with sensation and shortly after he knew which way to go. An internal compass, pointing him in the direction of wherever he could cause the most damage.

"Hope you like a little CCR," Ben said, turning on the stereo system and skipping forwarding till *Fortunate Son* started playing.

Ben turned up the volume and sped down the road.

4 WHEELS

Jon-Jon pulled over to the side of the road. His fuel gauge was teetering towards empty and he knew if he let go any longer they'd be pushing the van or leaving it by the wayside.

"What's the matter?" Scott called out as Jon-Jon stepped out of the truck.

"Just about on 'E'. You don't have a gas can on you, do you?"

"No. We're getting pretty low ourselves. Looks like a few cars up ahead, maybe they gassed up before they hit the road."

"That's what I was hoping. You don't have a hose do you?"

"I think that kid called Cups had it with him. We didn't really have much of anything with us except our clothes and shit."

"You think that Abdullah-whatever-the-fuck-his-name-is has anything?"

"He might. He was holed up with those people from the gas station. Maybe they grabbed some gas while they were there. It's what I would've done."

"Well, I'll go ask him. Keep your fingers crossed."

Abdul-Ba'ith sat idling several feet behind Scott and Judy's nearly demolished Hybrid. He'd given himself enough room to spin the truck around had he needed to. He sat gripping the wheel so tightly his knuckles went pale and when Jon-Jon approached the truck he did not get out. He simply rolled the window down half way.

Jon-Jon raised his hand out in a sort of waving gesture, hoping Abdul-Ba'ith would step out of the truck. With the glare on the windshield Jon-Jon could barely see inside.

"Hey, uh…Abda-Bath, you wouldn't happen to have a gas container on you, would you?"

"My name is Abdul-Ba'ith, not Abda-Bath, John. And no, I don't have any extra gas. We could use a refueling as well."

"Sorry, Abdul…ba—Can't I just call you Abdul?"

"Sure, but I really don't understand what is so difficult about my name."

"Well, Abdul, it just doesn't flow off my tongue, but I promise, if we live long enough to get to know each other I'll figure it out."

"Don't bother, we'll all be dead soon," Carrie spat.

"Fine," Abdul said, ignoring Carrie.

"Do you have a hose?"

"I honestly don't know what's in the back. This isn't my truck," Abdul-Ba'ith said, popping the latch and stepping out.

"We should just leave them," Carrie said.

They walked to the back of the truck and opened the rear door. Abdul-Ba'ith moved several bags of clothes, a bloodied bat, tire-iron, crowbar, and a few gallons of water out of the way so they could check the spare-tire compartment.

"No hose."

"Hey, at least we know you got a spare and a jack, and…yep, a donut under the spare. If I were you, I'd also take that other tire-iron out so it's handy."

"That I will," Abdul said, accepting a good suggestion.

"So I guess we'll drive up to this next section of cars and we'll start checking them. Might have to ditch the van and go with whatever has a full tank."

"Let's get to it then," Abdul-Ba'ith said, his eyebrows seeming to stiffen at the thought.

Jon-Jon walked back to the van and Abdul-Ba'ith hopped back in the truck to return to his statuesque pose behind the wheel. Carrie, having heard everything the two men said, still felt the need to ask what was going on. She bit her nails nervously as Abdul-Ba'ith went over it again. His tone was monotonous and though one might have found it almost soothing, Carrie just seemed to be more anxious. Abdul-Ba'ith thought about knocking her over the head with the tire-iron and kicking her out of the truck, but decided against it as the convoy started moving forward again.

Once they pulled in close to the next section of cars almost everyone got out and armed themselves. Jon-Jon, Eddie, Joseph, and Frankie went forward without hesitation. Chung-Hee hung back near the van with Chuck and they watched behind them and to the sides. Janice stayed in the van, indifferent to everything that was going on. Dawn walked toward Alexis and the children, smoking a cigarette as if her life depended on it. Passing her was Abdul-Ba'ith and Carrie, both carrying melee weapons from the back of the truck.

Scott and Judy climbed up on top of their Hybrid, which only increased their vantage point by a few feet, but it was still better than standing on the ground.

"Maybe we should join them, and look for another car?"

"I thought you liked this car?"

"I do—did—before it got all bloody. It's pretty gross, now, I don't even want to touch the handle to get in anymore."

"How about we take it to the car wash after they find some gas?"

"Even during the apocalypse you can still find some sarcasm. Unbelievable," Judy said, as she rolled her eyes.

"Believe it, babe. If it makes you feel any better, it's not my fault. My father was a sarcastic prick--"

"I know. It rubbed off."

"See anything?"

"No. Looks good from here."

"Yeah, me too. Want to go shopping for a new ride?"

"Why not? Maybe we can find a hearse?"

"Yeah, cause that wouldn't freak everyone else out," Scott smiled.

They laughed and climbed down from the car, hurrying to join the others.

The first set of cars had been abandoned, and the area seemed clear. Looking further down the road, however, they couldn't tell. The cars started to blur together. Maybe there was an accident up ahead, a pile up, followed by cars jamming up the open roadway. They'd know soon enough, so they returned focus to the task at hand—getting some gas, or a new set of wheels.

Jon-Jon opened a door on the driver's side of a Ford F-350. It was a Mechanical contractors truck—or so the logo on the side said so—

and he hoped there would be something of use inside; hopefully the key to the back rack toolbox in the bed of the truck. He rummaged under the seats, under the visors, and even the glove compartment. Whoever left the truck took their keys with them. Discouraged Jon-Jon slammed the door shut.

"No luck?" Dawn asked.

"Nope, and with our luck, there's a piece of hose in that box."

"Can you pry it open?"

"I could try, but I know it won't happen. An old friend of mine had one, he lost the key somehow and we tried to open it with a crowbar. We must've been at it for an hour before giving in a calling a locksmith over. The guy came and opened it in less time than we spent dicking around with it."

"No sense in crying about it. Let's keep looking," Scott suggested, "Someone had to of left their keys behind."

"I'm sure of it," said Jon-Jon, "and I'm sure if we go too far up we're going to find some of the people who left these cars behind, and they're gonna want to eat us."

"What else is new," said Frankie, moving on to the next car.

They found no keys in the next one but the trunk lever worked all the same. Eddie cautiously lifted if open with the bat he held in his hands. It was full of quickly packed bags of clothes, photo albums, and bottled water. There were a few boxes of granola bars, and couple of flashlights towards the back.

"I'll take the food and water back," Dawn offered.

She grabbed them and stared for a moment at the photo albums, wanting to open them, but at the same time wanting to run away from them. She felt pangs of grief just knowing that there were photographs in there at all—probably family memories of good days gone; birthday parties, holidays, picturesque walks in the park. She shoved the thought aside and made herself busy with the task at hand.

"Kind of feels like I'm stealing."

"Try not to think about it."

Eddie had walked forward to a black Lexus with tinted windows. The doors were locked. "Damn, I really wish the fucker who owned this left the keys."

"Hell yeah, we'd be riding in style," Joseph added.

Frankie pointed out the car seat in the back, and the smiles that

Eddie and Joseph wore wrinkled into frowns.

The next car was a clunker, rust around the wheel wells, lopsided bumper, and a different color door than the rest of the vehicle. The doors were open, and the key was in the ignition. The driver must've wanted someone to take it.

"Eddie, is that wood paneling on the side?"

"Yeah it is. I bet the guy who owned this heap had a mullet too."

"Man, I had a mullet when I was a kid," Jon-Jon said, looking embarrassed.

"That's fine, you obviously came to your senses."

Jon-Jon nodded approvingly and opened the door on the other side. They searched the car quickly and found very little of use. Frankie grabbed two lighters, Joseph found a small set of screwdrivers, and Eddie grabbed a backpack that had a bunch of kids stuff in it—some crayons, coloring books, Hot Wheels, and some action figures.

Judy had gone to the next vehicle before the others had finished rummaging through the clunker. It was an SUV, dark red, with a dent in the driver's side door. She peered through the back window. No one was inside and the back was full of luggage and some other bags. She went to open the back door but it wouldn't budge. She went to the driver's side and tried the door, it opened and she was able to pop the latch. She took a quick look around the interior. There was nothing of use in the front but checked the gas gauge—it was three quarters of the way full—and only a laptop in the back seat. By the time she returned to the back of the truck Scott was already searching through the luggage. Most of it was clothing, but he found a bottle of Tullamore Dew Irish Whiskey, a utility knife, a pack of new toothbrushes and an unopened box of toothpaste. He held up the toothbrushes and toothpaste to show Judy and she smiled.

"Now we can kiss each other again," he said jokingly.

"And just when I was getting used to the film on your teeth."

"That's not even funny. I think I'm gonna be sick."

"Shut up."

"Please tell me you found keys for this one. She's a keeper."

"Not yet. I gave a quick look but I don't see them. I was hoping they'd have an extra set in the luggage."

"Well, not in this guys case."

"Then check the lady's, and I'll check the visor and floor mats."

Scott rummaged through the other cases finding a camera, a carton of cigarettes, and a spare set of keys complete with the key for the truck.

"Score!"

"You found it?"

Scott shook the keys in his hand and said, "Told you I'd buy you a new car one day."

"Give me, I want to make sure it starts up."

Scott tossed the keys over to her and she hopped behind the wheel. The others gathered around while she started the truck.

"Damn, if I'd only gotten here first," Jon-Jon said.

"With this kind of luck, you'll find something soon," Scott reassured him.

"Shit, I hope so. I hate standing out here like this in the open. And looking inside these cars is just too fucking creepy."

"At least no one's in them."

"I'd bet one of these cars has a deader in it."

5 WE'VE GOT COMPANY

Walter took Barbara aside on the porch while Jeff went inside. Walter put his arm on her shoulder and she looked away to the dead things staggering closer to them.

"Sweetheart," he said, in that calm, cool, collected voice he always had, "you need to stop comparing yourself to your brother. You're both different people and years apart. You know, he wasn't always the good man you've known. He was a pain in the ass just like you once."

"I know, it's just…"

"Shh, just let it go. And please don't worry that you couldn't hit that thing out there. I know when you're life is on the line you won't even be able to think about it, you're just going to do it. You have a strength inside, and when you need it, it'll rise up like a phoenix."

"Yeah, okay."

"I mean it."

He pulled his baby girl closer and she nuzzled under his chin.

"Besides, it doesn't look like any of us are going to have a choice. These…things, whatever they are, don't want to quit. You're going to have to take one of them down sooner or later. Let's just hope it's later."

She hugged her old man, "Love you, dad."

"Love you too, sweetheart. Now let's get the hell in, these things give me the willies."

Jeff carefully placed his boots down on the rubber floor mat, being careful to not touch any wet spots that could've been blood. Walter and Barbara did the same. They all cleaned up in the kitchen using generous amounts of dish soap.

"Kills 99.9% of bacteria," Jeff said, "let's hope that .1% isn't a zombie bacteria."

"What was that?"

"I was saying the soap--"

"No, not that. That!"

"Oh, shit. They're banging at the door."

They ran to the front door. It was still locked. Walter walked up to the peephole and could see a duo of zombies banging and scraping at the door. One of them was wrapping its dead fingers around the doorknob and trying to turn it.

"Well, I'll be damned."

"What should we do?"

"Let's go to the windows," Jeff said, turning and running.

The windows had been boarded up, but Walter had suggested leaving a slit between some of the boards so that they could still see outside, without having to run up the second story.

"Look! They're drawing the attention of some of the wandering ones!"

"This isn't good at all," Walter huffed.

At that moment Laura came down the steps, the look of concern etched across her aging, yet still beautiful face, "What's going on?"

"We've got company, dear."

"Oh," is all she could manage, seeming to teeter on the steps. She looked as if she might loose her balance, but then she steadied herself on the railing.

"Why don't you just go back upstairs with the kids? Maybe you and Maria can put them to bed?"

"They're not tired, and if…if you're going to be making noise, then wouldn't that just wake them up? I think that might scare them, Walter."

"I think you're right. Well then just keep them from looking out the windows… and from coming downstairs."

Walter turned his attention back to the window and paused a moment on the steps before returning to her grandchildren.

"Jeff, we're going to open the front door while it's just the two of them and knock them the hell off the porch."

"What should I do?"

"Go grab my rifle. If they somehow get in, or overpower us, you need to put them down."

"In the head, right?"

"If you can manage, if not, maybe a knee, but maybe hitting them in the body will have enough kick to knock them back and give us a chance to finish the job."

Barbara nodded her head, and ran to get the rifle. Walter and his son suited up. The shovels were outside on the porch, and now needing them, Walter realized that he clearly didn't put them in the right place.

"Damn, the shovels are outside."

"It's okay, dad, we got the baseball bats in the closet."

"Yeah, but the shovel would've been better."

"You can always go outside and get it."

"Smartass."

Jeff grabbed the bats and Barbara had returned with the rifle. She stood holding it barefoot in the hallway while her father and brother readied themselves to open the door.

"Ready?"

"Nope. Check the peephole again."

"I'm opening the damned thing. Get ready," and Walter opened the door.

Jeff slipped passed and rammed the first zombie in the chest with the bat, knocking it back and to the side. Walter followed just behind as the next zombie was stepping forward, ready to enter the home. The would-be intruder was caught in the throat and Walter pushed him back. It's hand flailed to the side as it lost it's footing and was sent down the front steps tumbling down to the foot of the next zombie.

"Get your shoes on!" Walter yelled to Barbara.

She set the rifle down and slipped on her shoes in a flash, jumping back up to grab the rifle and head out the door. She stood in front of the door, bringing the rifle up to her shoulder and pulled a bead on the zombie leading the second wave.

Jeff was still struggling to knock his zombie off the porch.

"Need a hand?"

"No, I'm good, I think…"

Barbara ran over to him and smashed the butt of the gun into the side of the tall zombie's head, making a cracking noise. Jeff seized the opportunity and pushed with all of his might. The zombie was almost over the railing, then Barbara hit it again and over it went.

"Thanks, Barbie."

"Whatever, dweeb, go help dad."

Barbara moved back to her spot by the door and found the lead zombie again. Her father had already taken care of him, so she sought out the next closest zombie. She pulled a bead on a fat old lady zombie. She had curlers in her hair and the remnants of a moo-moo. Her lower half was covered in bites and rips. Her yellow fat hung out of the rips in her skin and Barbara almost vomited after seeing it. She held the bile back and pulled the trigger. Part of Fat Old Lady Zombie's head exploded, but she kept on walking.

"Fuck," Barbara said under her breath.

She took another shot and the big bitch dropped.

Jeff ran over to his father, "You okay?"

"My back is killing me, my allergies are acting up, and these damn zombies stink to high heaven."

"So…?"

"Shut up and hit one of them, will ya?"

Jeff swung at the knees of an approaching deader and knocked it right to the ground. The crack of rifle fire intermingled with the sounds of heads being shattered into piles of ruined mush.

6 SCAVENGERS

They continued to scavenge the cars on the road, every once and awhile someone would return back the convoy with whatever usable goods they found. They still found no hose, or spare gas canister. Jon-Jon was losing hope that they would find one, but the idea of getting a new vehicle was growing on him and when he laid eyes on a van that looked to be in good condition he forgot all about the damned hose.

"Look at this baby."

"What's with you and vans?"

"What do you mean? Vans are cool. I've always had a van, and I've never needed a hotel room, if you know what I mean," Jon said, grinning like a juvenile.

Eddie shook his head, "So we've been traveling in your sex den, is what you're saying."

"Well, not lately, but sure."

Eddie turned to his brother with a look of disgust, Joseph simply said, "It's better than riding in zombie goo."

"Look around back, while I check the driver's side?"

Eddie just nodded.

Jon-Jon peered inside the driver's side—it looked clear. Eddie looking around the back and side of the truck found nothing, so he called out to Jon-Jon, "Looks good."

Jon-Jon then opened the door, he smiled that it wasn't locked, and climbed in looking behind the seat to make sure there were no passengers—living or otherwise. It didn't smell like anything was dead inside either and it smelled a hell of a lot better than his old Astro Van. There was no key conveniently in the ignition so he checked all the usual spots; the visor was empty, under the floor mats was clear, cup holders were empty aside from pennies and nickels, the glove compartment looked like a file drawer, and just as he was about to give up he heard the sound of keys jingling as they fell off the seat he was sitting on.

"Son of a gun," he said to himself, snatching the keys up.

"Got 'em?" Joseph asked, disbelievingly.

"Hells yeah. Look at this sweet ride."

"Man, I'd rather be rolling around in that Lexus."

"Keep looking."

Scott came over and threw in his two cents, "If we don't need it, we should leave it, and get the hell out of here. I'd rather get as far north as we can, and then go car shopping."

"I wasn't serious, man," Joseph said, "I want out of here as soon as possible. I was just saying."

"No, I know, hell I'd rather find a Hummer, but as long as it's gassed and good to go I'll hop in and push the pedal to the metal."

"So are we good to go then?"

"I don't see why not. Unless we need anything else, we should keep moving."

Eddie stepped closer to the others and said, "How is everyone on food and water? So long as the coast is clear it can't hurt to find out what we have and search a few more cars to see if we can find it."

Scott nodded in agreement, "Sounds good. Let's tell the others to at least move forward, though. Anyone want to run back and give the word?"

"I'll do it, I want to move the van up so I can swap out my shit."

"Ask everyone to check if they need anything," Scott called after.

Jon-Jon threw out a thumbs-up and kept walking.

Chung-Hee and Chuck—an odd couple if there ever was one—hopped back in the van as Jon-Jon had notified them of the pending trade-in.

"Do you mind I continue riding with you?" Chunge-Hee asked.

"Not at all, man, unless you want out of course. Having everyone taking shifts driving, and just having people to talk to is great."

"I agree. I hate taking long trips by myself. I tend to get pretty sleepy after an hour or so in the car."

"Damn," Chuck chimed in, "maybe you shouldn't be taking any shift then!"

The three of them laughed at that.

Jon-Jon had pulled the van to the grass median and drove it to close proximity of his new van. The three of them got out and started carrying over what few supplies they had left. They were able to bring it all in one shot.

Dawn had met them as they were putting the supplies in the back of the new van and she had acquired some new things from scavenging through the cars.

"You can shop just about anywhere, huh?"

"You better believe it."

The rest of the convoy shortly followed after.

Alexis walked over to Joseph. She smiled warmly at him and he couldn't help but smile back. His cheeks grew warm and reddened a touch.

"How are they holding up?"

"They're a bunch of tough little kids, but they're looking pretty beat up."

"Anything I can do to help?"

"Actually, yeah…if you guys are still looking around for stuff, can you keep your eyes open for kids vitamins, maybe some kids medicines, Pedialyte maybe. You know, stuff like that."

"Sure, I'll keep my eyes open. How about you? Do you need anything?"

"A cozy pair of slippers, pj's and a bottle of Riesling."

"I know you're kidding, but I can probably find those before I come across the stuff for the kids."

"Then don't let me stop you."

Eddie followed his brother as he scavenged forward, looking for any number of the things that everyone needed, but he was more concerned with finding something for Alexis.

"Don't loose your head," Eddie said.

"I'm not man, I'm just…ya know, I want to get this shit and get out of here."

"I know. I do too, but we can find your girlfriend some slippers when we're someplace she can actually were them, you know?"

"Yeah, yeah you're right. Fuck it. Let's go."

"Good, we've been at this for an hour and all these empty cars are giving me the fucking creeps. Big time."

"Seriously."

"Hey…"

"Yeah?"

"Can I ask you something without you thinking I'm crazy?"

"Too late."

"All right. It's happened a few times now, and since we've been looking through these cars it's happened a few times more."

"What's happened?"

"I think I'm seeing ghosts, man. But not just seeing, like I'm feeling them too. It's really fucking weird. It's like a cold shiver runs right through me, or I'll see like a shadow move that shouldn't be there. It's not like I'm seeing a ghost, like Sixth Sense or something, but more like a feeling, like I just know."

"You're freaking me out even more now. You know I fucking hate ghosts. Mom used to talk about that shit all the time with Grandma when she was alive. I wouldn't be able to sleep for days. And now you're going to start with it."

"Do you think I'm losing it?"

"Yes. No, well I don't know man, I'm not seeing anything weird, except for the zombies."

"I knew I should've kept my mouth shut."

"I believe you, but I just don't want to think of anymore freaky shit. Zombies. Ghosts. What else, man? What's next?"

"Gremlins."

"Gremlins would be a walk in the park. Shit, they could be pets. All you have to do is follow two rules: no eating after midnight, and don't get them wet. How hard is that?"

"You guys talking about Gremlins again?" Chung-Hee asked.

"You know it."

"Dude, give me a Gremlin Apocalypse over a Zombie Apocalypse any day."

"Amen."

Abdul-Ba'ith stood beside his truck stretching his legs. "You should stretch, too," he suggested to Carrie.

"No, thanks."

"We'll be driving for a while. It's not good for circulation to sit so long without doing some stretching every now and again."

"How about fuck off."

"How about you go find a vehicle and follow behind the rest of us?"

"Is that a threat?"

"Take it as you will, but if you end up getting a blood clot because you refuse to get out of the car and stretch your legs you are threatening my life, Alexis's life, and the children's lives. So, please get off your big ass and stretch out for a few minutes if you plan to keep driving with us."

Carrie didn't respond, but she stared at Abdul-Ba'ith with an incredulous look etched across her face as she got out of the car and walked away.

Alexis looked at Abdul-Ba'ith and asked, "Do you think she'll find another ride?"

"Sadly, no. I'm sure she's going to hide behind a car, stretch, and then come back to us."

"How has she made it this long without someone killing her?"

"I'd say luck, so maybe it will be good to have her with us."

"Can we strap her to the roof?"

"If she keeps up her wonderful attitude I'll figure something out."

Sure enough, Carrie had come back. She didn't look at anyone in the truck, but climbed in and sat down.

Jon-Jon, sitting comfortably in his new van worked his way to the grass median where he then led the convoy to the other side of the highway. It looked much easier to navigate then the right side and hopefully it would take them past whatever had caused the traffic jam to begin with.

7 LOOSE END

He felt alive, even though he was anything but. The wind whipped his hair around like blades of grass in an open field. His arm hung out the window, and he sat slumped in his chair as if it were a throne fit for the King himself. He had a belly full of the darkest energy that surely ever existed. He thought it felt a lot like a belly full of whiskey on a cold night, but there was a hell of lot more to it than that.

There was someone, or something, inside him. In some ways he felt like a limb, or part of a hive, he thought. He didn't feel like a puppet on a string or anything like that, but he knew he was tapped into some serious shit. Maybe the Devil himself was taking a liking to him.

Whatever it was seemed to know everything that was on his mind. And he too could feel parts of conversations, emotions, but it was all just a soft noise in the background of his mind. Questions were answered with a sudden understanding. Pain became pleasure. Feeling his own body going through the early stages of physical death simply felt like the sparks that would start a fire.

He could feel, as if by some form of autonomy, where the living and the dead were—an internal compass for them both. It was with that knowledge that he knew what streets to turn down and what direction to take to get to his destination. He wanted to find the one that got away. And after he was done with her, he was going to track down those other self righteous sacks of meat and rend them each to a slow death between his teeth.

***

Days earlier…

Sarah wasn't entirely sure how she did it. Or how she even had the courage to try, but it was that or it was letting that sick fuck have his way with her and then kill her. Her body ached from the fight, and even worse was the pain she felt in her ankle. The pain burned brightly, traveling to her knee. The way she hobbled into the woods, putting all her wait on the pad of her foot and off her heel was alleviating the pressure a touch, but come tomorrow her entire foot, and probably her leg would hurt.

She knew she couldn't keep this up much longer. Jumping off the roof saved her from that maniac, but she now had the attention of several deaders that were following her into the thick of the woods. She was moving quicker than them for now, but she wouldn't for much longer. The pain was dominating her, and all she wanted to do was sit down and nurse her wounds. The dead didn't think like that, if they thought at all. They didn't get tired, and they sure as shit didn't care about their wounds. As slow as they were they would never need to stop and catch their breath.

The moon was obscured from the thick branches overhead and all Sarah could see were thin slivers of light on the edges of the trees. Her eyes had adjusted to the dark, but this deep in and the moon might as well have not existed. Her lungs burned, her leg throbbed, and she just wanted to give in but the sounds of the deaders crunching leaves underfoot spurred her forward again.

As she trotted painfully through territory unknown, images of Boone and Milah flashed through her mind. Though her and Milah had been friends for a few years, they both took to Boone quickly as if they'd known him far longer than the few days they really did. Despite it being the end of the world they made the best of it. Laughs were few and far between but when they did occur they were sincere and contagious. She missed them both dearly, but the loss of her friend Milah was devastating. It numbed her, and wedged a ball in her throat. Her eyes were wet with tears of pain, and if she ever survived the night she would weep unending for her friend.

When Sarah thought all was lost and her legs were giving out and tripping her up more than they were carrying her forward she lie on the ground weighing out the benefit of getting up and pushing forward again. She would just collapse again. The sounds of the dead behind her had softened. Perhaps some had decided to go back, and the others were slowly catching up to her. Whatever the reason, she still could not see a reason to push herself up. Then she noticed a light on in a window just past the edge of the woods. She made it. She was at the end, and there was a light. Then the light went out and she got up to find what house it came from.

She hobbled out of the woods and onto a street. She stood at the corner of Werrlein Ave and Mathis Street watching the windows on the second floor for signs of life. Most of the homes were boarded up on the first floors, and some on the second as well. The light in the window she saw was definitely from the second floor. She knew it wasn't the first house, but that it was certainly one of the first few.

Looking and listening for signs and sounds of life only revealed to her the sounds of the dead closing in. Their moans mixed in with the crunching of leaves and twigs. She turned to her right at the sound of something dragging on the street—it was a deader with a mangled foot that dragged behind it as it walked. With each step the ruined limb scraped against the blacktop, and she soon realized that the scraping noise was the sound of its bone scraping the black top. There was no shoe, sock, and barely any skin left. She wanted to throw up, but instead she decided to start screaming.

"Help! Please help, I know you're there!"

She moved down the street, screaming herself raw.

"Help you coward! I can't run anymore, please fucking help me!"

Her eyes were wide with terror, she was bordering on madness now.

"JUST LET ME IN! I'm not bit. I'm alive! Fucking help me!"

She had almost lost her voice when a window opened and a man yelled down to her, "Jesus Christ, lady, shut the fuck up. You're going to bring them all over here."

"Let me in, please. I'm begging you," she cried.

"If you're bit, or bleeding, I will shoot you dead."

"Fine."

She made her way over to the house. The man closed the window and ran down the stairs to open the door. She nervously moved the small front porch as she could hear movement behind the door. The man was pushing stuff aside. A barricade, she figured. She could hear him grunting as something slid slowly across the floor. Just down the street came the scraping sound of the dead man and his ruined foot.

Scrrtttch... Scrrtttch... Scrrtttch...

Sarah wanted to scream. To pull her hair and scream like a woman gone mad with clumps of hair and scalp in her hands.

Scrrtttch... Scrrtttch... Scrrtttch...

Dead things stumbled out of the woods. They began to moan for her. The sounds of teeth clacking together.

Clack-Click-Clak-Clik...

Scrrtttch... Scrrtttch... Scrrtttch...

"Come on, come on," she whimpered.

When the door finally opened she could swear it was as loud as a gunshot. A man with a gaunt face and a week's worth of stubble opened the door and peered out. His eyes were wild and he held a small pistol in his hand.

"Have you been bitten? Scratched?"

"No. I swear. You can check me when I come in, just please…"

"I won't hesitate to kill you," he warned.

"Fine," she said, pushing her way in.

"Help me barricade the door again."

She hobbled over and helped the man push a heavy bureau against the door. She doubted she was much help, and then they moved some smaller pieces of furniture around the sides of it.

"Now, come on, upstairs. We have to get their attention away from the house."

"How?"

"Just come on."

The man took the stairs two at a time and Sarah did her best to keep up but all she wanted to do was collapse. She stumbled at the top of the stairs, catching herself in the doorway as the man opened the window.

"Get down," he told her.

She squatted, and a sharp pain traveled up her leg from the way she positioned herself. "What are you doing?" She asked in a pained voice through gritted teeth.

The man grabbed an empty glass bottle. Sarah thought it was an empty bottle of vodka, but she couldn't tell for sure in the darkness of the room. "I have to distract them, otherwise they'll start trying to get in here. This worked before, and I hope it will again."

He through the bottle out the window, arching it over the corner of the roof of the adjacent house, and hoping it smashed into the street. He held his breath for a moment and heard the telltale shatter of the bottle. He grinned in delight and then poked his head just above the windowsill to look out. He couldn't see if they'd gone towards the bottle or continued toward his home.

"Can't see shit. Stay here."

She nodded, thankful for not having to move. She sat down, putting her back against the wall, as the man stepped past her and quietly moved down the stairs. He stood at the bottom of the steps listening intently to hear if anything was coming up the steps or scratching at the door. He heard nothing and assumed his distraction worked. He was happy there were only a few of them outside. Any more and they would probably have drowned out the noise that the bottle made. Their moans and grunts alone weren't very loud, but coupled in the dozens and they were deafening.

"Looks like we're in the clear," he said as he came back into the room.

Sarah had already fallen asleep.

8 EXPECT DELAYS

The convoy moved forward at a slow pace. Navigating through the vehicles had become trickier and tighter the farther up they went. The tight spaces made everyone nervous and on edge. Eddie had become the annoying backseat driver and Jon-Jon was doing his best to keep his cool, but he wasn't sure how much longer he'd be able to do it.

"How's the shoulder looking?" Eddie asked from behind them.

"If you can't see it then I can't see it. You're practically in my fucking lap."

"Sorry man. I'm just getting claustrophobic."

Dawn asked, "Maybe you should close your eyes?"

"Then I'll just get motion sickness from all the zigzagging."

"Shit. I thought you were a tough guy," Jon-Jon started to laugh.

"Give me an Xbox controller and I'll kick anybody's ass."

Then Frankie chimed in, "Bullshit you will."

Dawn screamed. Jon-Jon hit the brakes.

"What is it?"

"Inside the car! Look!"

"What? Where?"

"There!"

Jon-Jon followed Dawn's finger to a smaller accident in the abandoned roadway. There were three cars, two had badly sandwiched the one. The windshield was blown out and semi-shattered across the hood. From the angle they were at Jon-Jon could see right into the car and what he saw made him sick to his stomach.

Dawn brought her hand down but they both remained staring. Eddie peered between the two of them trying to pinpoint what they were looking at when he found it he too felt sick. There was a deader pinned inside the car. A seatbelt held her in place, but even if she figured out how to get out of it, the car was so tightly smashed together that she would probably still be unable to get out. He skin looked leathery from the sun and her dried blood looked black. She must've broken her nose and her smile on the steering wheel because most of her lower face was covered in the black blood, unless it just wasn't there at all.

"Should we put her out of her misery?"

"It's not a wounded animal, Ed, that's a fuckin' deader. And by the looks of it, she ain't going anywhere."

"Seems fucked up to just leave her though."

"I'd rather be fucked up than risking my ass for the humane treatment of deaders."

"You're right, fuck it. Let's go."

Jon-Jon released the break and pushed down gently on the gas. The other vehicles in the convoy paused to figure out what they had seen, but quickly followed.

Every time Janice closed her eyes she traveled back in time to the moment when her world went to hell and her soul was irrevocably shattered. It just wasn't fair. She shouldn't have to have outlived any of her children, or her husband, but certainly not her two little babies. Each one was a miracle.

She was aging and it had been years since she gave birth to Joseph, over a decade. Her doctor warned her of all the possible outcomes of a woman her age giving birth, but she didn't care. She was a mom, and her two kids were growing into men and ready to leave home. She couldn't, and really didn't want to go back to work, so after some much needed convincing on her husbands behalf they decided to have a child, which turned into two.

The absence in her heart ached terribly and all she could remember of them were their horrific and bloody ends. The good times were hard to remember now. Not because she couldn't remember them, but because the scarring of her mind that those last horrid images caused would never heal, the wounds would just reopen with every blink of her eyes.

She took comfort in knowing her eldest sons were surviving through it all. That she had a good hand in raising them right and making sure they could take care of themselves. They made her proud, but they could not fill the holes in her heart that were slowly killing her. She felt as numb and as dead to the world as she had felt that first day. There would be no getting better, no getting over it. She would feel this way to the end, and that's why she knew the next time she had the chance to she would get too close to the deaders and let them do what they do best, and take a big bite out of her. It was suicidal, but she didn't think the good lord would consider it suicide. In her mind it was no worse than smoking while dying of terminal cancer.

Joseph sat with his arm around his mother and his mind succumbing to its own machinations. He too couldn't stop thinking of his much younger siblings, or his father. Much of his thoughts were of regrets. He regretted how he spent so much time involved in his own life and not nearly enough time playing with his young brother and sister. He was too busy growing up and butting heads with his father to pay them much attention. He had a full schedule of classes and worked most nights, when he was doing neither he was usually found studying or seeing how many beers he could drink in a night without throwing up.

Unlike his mother, however, he wanted to live. He wanted to make up for what he considered to be his shortcomings somehow. He wanted redemption. He wanted to keep his mother safe for his father, to let him know he could be responsible…that he could be a man. He wanted to be there for his brother. To be at his side no matter what, just like they always said they'd be. There was nothing to get in the way this time, and if he couldn't be there for him now, at the end of the fucking world, then what kind of brother was he?

When they were younger, and all they had to do was go to school, be home in time for dinner, and after dinner to be home before ten they always had time for each other. Hell, they were best friends growing up. They shared comics, cards, toys, everything. They went to the clay pits on their bicycles; walked the train tracks all the way up to the trestle that overlooked The Devil's Tail; played wall ball, and even stayed up some nights to watch the late night movie, which usually consisted of a monster or giant bug movie, like The Creature From the Black Lagoon, or Empire of the Ants.

Those were the days, and they never seemed further away than they did now.

Jon-Jon was able to steer the van, and consequently the convoy, out of the mess of vehicles on the road and onto the shoulder. He drove up the shoulder as far as he could until having to take to the side of the road, which was much bumpier, but seemed to be clear as far as his eyes could see.

Eddie was still leaning forward between Jon-Jon and Dawn, but was now starting to feel sick from the bumpy ride. He couldn't focus on anything beyond the windshield and it was giving him a headache. Fuck it, he thought. Jon-Jon was more than capable of driving the van and getting everyone closer to the coast. Eddie just wanted to preoccupy himself with something to do. If he wasn't doing something his mind would wander through the days that led up to today and they were all pretty bad. He thought it was funny how you could have a life full of good times, but only focus on the bad ones. Maybe if good times left scars, he'd be more inclined to remember them.

He moved to the back, almost falling over Chung-Hee's leg, to sit next to his brother and mother. He leaned over the back of the seat, looking for his backpack and rifled out his notebook and pencil. He doubted he'd be able to write anything down with the van bouncing around as it was, but at the very least he could read over his journal entries from the days before. He was never much for writing, but he figured it would be an okay way to keep track of events, and at the least, days. It was as much a calendar as it was a journal, and as he opened it up he saw an entry that was just the date, the time, and a barely legible scribble that read, 'fuck this bullshit.'

Those three words pretty much summed up his thoughts on the whole end-of-the-world-by-zombies thing that was going on. Then again, that was pretty much his motto in life. When things got to real, to serious, it was bullshit. When girlfriends got to serious it was time to walk away. When work started looking like a career it was time to hand in his two weeks.

As he flipped through his notebook he traveled back in time and could see his words on the page transform into a crystal clear memory of the days that blurred into one long, unending, motherfucker of a day. He flipped all the way to the beginning of the notebook—day one. When he wrote it it was nighttime, and technically it might've been the second day, because he couldn't recall what time he actually wrote it. He stared at it for a moment, then he realized he didn't want to go back there. He didn't want to remember any of the shit that had happened. So he closed the book, closed his eyes, and did his best not to cry.

He folded his arms and faked trying to sleep as the tears silently slid down his face.

9 WHEN SARAH MET JIM

The man woke her up by putting an ice pack to her cheek. Startled, she jumped as the beginnings of a scream died in her throat as she came to realize where she was. The man backed away, immediately regretting waking her the way he did. Not so much because it startled her, but because she almost screamed. And if she had screamed, it was a good possibility this pain in his ass's voice would carry all the way outside and rouse up some of those dead fuckers that he'd been doing his best to stay clear of.

She took the ice pack and quietly said, "Thanks."

He nodded, and then took a seat on the floor close to her. He looked her over carefully, staring at her scratches and bruises as best he could in the dark. She looked at him, knowing what he was about to ask, and beat him to the chase, "I wasn't bit. I already told you that."

"And I'm supposed to take your word?"

"Then just let me catch my breath and I'll be on my way."

"If that's what you want to do I won't stop you, but just because I'm trying to be safe and smart about this doesn't mean I want to see you go out there and get yourself killed."

"How can I prove to you I wasn't bit? Those things didn't lay a hand on me—and I'm not stripping down for anyone!"

"Then tell me what happened. Tell me how you got to be out running around in the woods."

She stared at him for what felt like a long moment, but in all actuality was only the time it took to take a breath, "I was with a bigger group. There was a whole bunch of us. Most of us had been surviving on the road and meeting up with others and joining up and blah blah blah. A bunch of us wanted to head into Titan City--"

"Why the fuck would you go into the city?"

"A lot of us have, had—whatever—family there. With nowhere to go it seemed like a good idea. And it still does. My mom and dad live there. I talked to them just a few days ago and they said things were getting better. Anyway, we made it to a school, which is where I ran from. There was a psycho son of a bitch that ended up traveling with us. Seemed like a normal guy. Then he killed two of m-my friends, and…and he t-tried to kill me too. I jumped off the roof—that's where we were—and ran for the woods. I heard him shoot at me, but he must've missed. The building was surrounded with those things, those dead bastards, and I guess some of them followed me. I must've sprained my ankle from the jump or maybe in the woods, and that's where I got all these cuts, and well some of the bruises were from that fucking psycho, but this is all from running in the woods. And those things are slow, but when you don't know where you're going, and you can barely breathe or see or run they keep up just fine."

"Jesus Christ lady, that's a lot to take in. Why don't we get you bandaged up? I got a fist aid kit in the bathroom and I know I have a wrap somewhere for your ankle. Then maybe drink something and get some rest."

"Sounds great."

The man held out his hand after getting up and helped Sarah to her feet. He showed her to the bathroom, got the first aid kit for her and backed away.

"I'll let you do your thing. Just try to be quiet. I'll be back over in my room by the window if you need me."

"Okay, thanks, uh…sorry, what's your name?"

"Jim. And you?"

"Sarah."

Jim went back to the window and peered out. There wasn't much more action than usual on the street which allowed him to relax a bit. He still wasn't sure about this girl—about Sarah—she seemed sincere enough, but how could he know for certain that she wasn't somehow infected with whatever turns people into these zombies.

Jim was fortunate enough to have been home when everything started happening. When the first news reports occurred he thought they were faked. For most of the first day he thought it was a joke, but by the end of day one it was everywhere. The coverage was nonstop and far more engaging than Pawn Stars or Law & Order.

No one could say for definite what was happening, but as the days went on and the situation continued to degenerate two sides seemed to emerge from the chaos: Atheists, and Theists. Both groups only touted their beliefs and found new reasons for division instead of unison. The media chose sides as well and any real information was lost in the noise as the great debate of whether or not this cataclysmic event was God's will or some sort of infectious disease.

Faith in things unseen was always tricky for Jim to wrap his head around. He thought it made sense for some sort of God or Deity to exist but just couldn't get straight with all the ritual aspects of worshipping one. He loved science, believed in aliens, but he knew there was a limit to what to science could explain. Even now, at the end of times, he couldn't pick a side of course except for the side of the living.

Sarah peeled her clothes from her body and turned the shower on. She stepped in and didn't care a bit that the water was freezing—she could barely feel it. She grabbed the soap and scrubbed at her body as hard and as fast as she could. This wasn't time for a relaxing shower, no, this was time to get in and get out. She didn't know this Jim guy at all and had no reason to trust he wouldn't barge in and try anything but she needed to get clean. She was done in under four minutes and dry in less than one. She wrapped herself tightly in the towel and stared at her dirty clothes. She didn't want to put them back on, and she didn't want to step out in a towel.

She bit her lip in indecision for a few moments and then opened the door a crack and whispered, "Jim."

No reply, so she did it again, "Hey Jim!"

Jim came running, "What's the matter?"

"I…uh, just wanted to know if you had any extra clothes you could lend me. I decided to shower off."

"I doubt any of my pants will fit you but let me take a look I'm sure I can find something."

He returned a few minutes later with an old black t-shirt that read

Arson on it red, a pair of sweatpants and a pair of socks.

"Here you go. This stuff doesn't really fit me to well anymore," he said, patting his slight beer belly, "but it should do the trick for ya. Probably going to be big, but it's all I got."

"Thanks, I'm sure they'll be fine."

She put the clothes on and sure enough they were big on her. The shirt would've been something she might've worn to bed, but she was swimming in the pants. She pulled the string as tight as it would go and double knotted it. The socks were loose too and dropped down past her ankles. It was better than nothing, she thought, and stepped out of the bathroom.

She walked over to Jim who returned to the window. "Any new developments," she asked softly.

"Nope. Looks okay out there."

"Good. Thanks again for opening the door. I'd probably be dead right now…walking around like those things."

"Your welcome. How do the clothes fit?"

"They're a little big, but they'll do."

"So, ummm, what do we do now, how does this work?"

"What do you mean?"

"Well, do you have a plan? Have you thought about what you're going to do?"

"Not really. If you want me to take off, I'll go--"

"Sorry, I didn't mean it like that. I just—I haven't seen anybody in days, if you're part of a larger group it makes sense to stay with them. I've been too scared to leave and didn't know what to do."

"You're from around here, right? If you know where the school is maybe we can drive over there in the morning and see what's going on."

"Yeah, yeah we can do that. You don't mind me coming along with you?"

"Not at all. The more the merrier."

"Good maybe we should rest up and get some sleep? I have a futon you can sleep on in my computer room next to the bathroom."

"Doubt I'll be able to sleep much."

"Do you want to try getting to your group now, then?"

"I'm not sure. I'm…I don't want to see that bastard again."

"I understand, but maybe some of your friends have found out what's happened—or maybe someone else is in danger."

"I thought of that, but I don't see how we can get back into the school. The place is surrounded by them—mostly."

"What do you mean mostly?"

"They aren't around the fence—at least they weren't. They were mostly just around the building."

"So we could climb the fence and get inside then?"

"I dunno, maybe."

"Do you want to try for it or do you want to rest?"

"I guess we can try for it, but if you're going to stick with us you might want to pack as much of your shit as you can. And any food and water you have left."

"Okay, I'll start packing up my stuff. Why don't you rest up in the meantime—give me an hour or so."

With that, Jim went into his closet and found an old backpack, a gym bag, and the only suitcase he owned—which was so busted up it didn't look like it would survive another trip, even if it were just down the road.

Sarah went into the computer room and curled up on the futon. She didn't think she'd fall asleep, but she was so exhausted she was out before she knew it.

10 SPECIAL OCCASION

Walter walked to his bedroom, every bone in his body ached. His lower back felt like it had been stung by several bees and his left leg twitched from a numbing nerve that he refused to have a doctor look at. He was an old man, with an old man's body and he didn't need some damned Indian doctor telling him that and then expecting a twentyfive dollar copay. A good night's rest was all he needed, or at least it used to be. Nowadays nothing seemed to work, and the pains never seemed to go away. That was life, or maybe just the slow end of it.

In the corner of the bedroom was an old rocking chair. Laura bought it when she was pregnant with Barbara. Walter sanded and stained it more times than anything else in the home. Laura knitted scarves and hats in it now and Walter would sometimes read and sip a few fingers of brandy on special occasions. It sat in the corner with a thin ribbon of moonlight glistening along its curves. Beside it was a small nightstand. In it were Laura's knitting needles and a few bundles of yarn in a wicker basket. Behind that was a bottle of Walter's favorite brandy, Ararat, aged almost as long as the chair, and a simple, yet elegant snifter.

He bent down, back creaking, and wrapped his weathered hands around the nape of the bottle's neck. He set it on the nightstand and grabbed the snifter. This wasn't really a special occasion, certainly not a time for sitting idly on an old chair with a brandy, but he was alive, his family was alive, and that was something special on these new days. Every day alive was now a special occasion and Walter could drink to that.

The pour was slow but shaky and Walter clanked the bottle against the glass a few times. The snifter was three fingers deep and the bottle was more than half full. He hoped he had as many days as the bottle had fingers deep. He sniffed the Armenian brandy, gently swishing it around the glass and put it to his lips. The dry skin of his chapped lips rejoiced as the caramel colored fluid flowed behind his teeth.

It gave a little burn on the way down but all in all it was smooth and velvety and felt right at home when it reached bottom. Walter sat down and gently rocked himself in the chair. He took another sip as he stared out the window. The blinds were open only a crack, but that was all he needed to see that all was not well.

Walter looked around the room and everything in it brought a memory to his mind; the day they bought the place; the day they moved in; the day they finally bought some proper furniture. He thought about some of their old friends and how most of them were dead or sunning it up in Florida.

He was a dinosaur. Extinct, but unlike those once rulers of the world, he knew it.

He took another sip of the Ararat.

Laura crept into the room. The door opened smoothly—Walter oiled the hinges religiously—and for a moment Walter didn't notice her standing there looking at him, but when he did he smiled.

"What's the occasion?"

"We're alive."

"For how much longer?"

"Our days were over a long time ago. I'm more worried about our grandkids."

Laura said nothing and gracefully closed the distance from the doorway to the rocking chair.

She put her hand on his. Walter patted his knee and Laura sat down in his lap, resting her head on his shoulder. Their wrinkled skin was illuminated by the light of the moon as they gently rocked. Walter was never much for the mushy stuff and he certainly wasn't one for tears, but despite was he wasn't much for the tears started to run down the hard lines of his face.

"I wish I could tell you that our grandkids are going to be

okay…that they're going to have a future, but I can't. If there is a God and a heaven he calls home, then maybe we'll all be happy there when this mess is all over."

"There is a God, sweetie, there is. I know there is. I just don't know why he's doing this, or letting this happen. I—I just don't know…"

"Guess we're going to find out, beautiful. It's been one hell of a ride. I've loved you more than life itself. You made every day a special occasion. You gave me a son, and a daughter, and your love."

"And you've given me yours," she said, her words turning into soft sobs.

Walter's shirt grew wet with her tears and all he could do was rub her back and keep the chair rocking.

The children were asleep. Jeff and Maria bookended them in bed and when they were sure they were asleep they slid out of bed and tiptoed out of the bedroom. Once Jeff was in the hallway and Maria was a few steps ahead, he gently closed the door. Thankfully his father was a nut about oiling hinges and the door made no noise as it was drawn to a close.

"I can't believe they went to sleep so quickly," Jeff said.

"Don't expect it every time."

"I won't. I figure once they see what's outside--"

"Why would they ever have to see it?"

"We can't shelter them from it forever."

"We can try."

"And we will, but that don't mean it's gonna happen like that."

"All we have to do is shelter them long enough for this all to get cleaned up."

"This again? Really? We are on our own, Maria, why can't you see that?"

"The military will get this under control soon enough. They're equipped to deal with shit like this."

"No one is equipped to deal with shit like this. If there's any military force left they sure as hell can't do it alone. We need to pull our own weight. We need to be our own army, our own protectors."

"Come on, guys, give it a fucking rest," Barbara chimed in as Jeff and Maria made their way downstairs.

"Sorry, Barb," Maria said.

"Shut up, Barbie, you know I'm right."

"Can you stop with the Barbie bullshit? You know you are the sole reason I never played with them damned things, and as a result knew nothing of fashion."

"You're a trendsetter, stop complaining."

"So, is all quiet?"

"They're still out there. They're walking. Roaming, I guess. Some of them look like they might come this way, but most of them seem to be following the others. I haven't really been able to make any sense of it."

"I don't think we ever will."

"I'll see how we're doing with food and water. Where's the flashlight?"

"Should be…right there," Barbara pointed

Maria grabbed the flashlight from the coffee table and headed to the kitchen.

"Where are Mom and Dad?"

"Upstairs."

"What're they doing?"

"How the fuck should I know? Probably having some alone time."

"Alone time?"

"Don't be gross."

"I'm just kidding. Can't I crack a joke?"

"No."

"How you holding up?"

"Great, you know, aside from the fucking zombies."

Jeff couldn't help but smile at that.

"I'm okay. I think I might be getting a bit stir crazy, though."

"You can always go for a jog."

"Mr. Funny guy tonight."

"Yeah, you know it."

"How 'bout you? How are you doing?"

"I'm just worried about the kids. I can take care of myself, I think Maria would do okay, but if the shit got heavy and we had to get out of here? I'm terrified one of those things would get ahold of one of the kids."

"You can't think about that."

"Easier said than done, but shut it, here comes the boss."

Maria came back from the kitchen.

Barbara asked, "Well?"

"Not too good."

"What do you mean?"

"Well, we have plenty of stuff to eat and drink, but there's just too many of us for it to last long. There's a lot of us."

"Give us some numbers."

"Eight cases of water. Six gallons of water. Four bottles of Ginger Ale. Two cases of Hi-C, plus all the water we bottled and filled the tubs with, which I have no idea how to count, but if we get to that level I'm sure it's going to be gross."

"Well, that gives us a week, right?"

"Not if we use some of it to cook with."

"But we still have running water."

"Today we do. Tomorrow…?"

"No variables, please. Food?"

"Food we're pretty good on I think. We have those two metal pantries full of canned foods and boxed pasta. I'd say at least three weeks till were down to nothing. Of course, that's eating mac & cheese and plain spaghetti."

"We don't need gourmet."

"We can always start scouting for food from the neighbors that have taken off."

"Barbie the scavenger."

"Fuck, bro, I'm being serious."

"I know, and it's a good idea. If we can, we should start tomorrow."

"Are you serious?"

"Sadly yes. I know how my kids eat, and if we are that low on water we might as well strike now before things get any worse."

"Dad's going to want to weigh in on that one."

"I'm sure he will, and I'm sure he'll agree."

"Yeah, probably…anything else Mar?"

"Well if you guys are going to visit the neighbors things like toilet paper, soap, and coffee couldn't hurt."

"Noted."

"Hey, where's your dad?"

Barbara smirked, "Alone time."

"Don't be gross, sis."

"Me?"

11 ONLY IN DREAMS

The convoy moved along the road swiftly. They were fortunate enough to hit a decent stretch of road, where congestion had broken up and accidents were minimal. Abandoned cars were fewer and fewer and therefore the convoy was able to move quicker. Jon-Jon stayed focused on driving. His eyelids were heavy and he badly wanted to sleep, but he was able to push it aside and continue driving.

Dawn on the other hand had fallen asleep and her cheek rested on the window, leaving a greasy spot as her face moved up and down along with the rhythm of the van. Her sleep was full of dreams— intermingled memories cutting across the movie screen of her mind with every vivid color and detail usually reserved for reality.

She was at her father's wake; standing at her mother's side, staring at the sleek black coffin that snuggly fit her father's large frame. Beautifully arranged flowers were scattered all over the room, desperately trying to remind people that life was full of wonder and color and beauty—not just black suits and black dresses and pale faced widows with weeping daughters.

Dawn held her mother's hand. It was cold and dry, but it squeezed back with all the strength it could. Her father looked asleep, almost like he was smiling. Dawn saw that smile on her father's face so often. Usually as he slept on the couch after a few beers on the weekends when he wasn't working.

She approached the casket. Light glistened on its black surface like the nighttime surf of the ocean. Gentle rippling waves crashing against the smooth sand. This wasn't her father. It couldn't be. The gentle waves grew rough…

…and now she was standing on the beach. Her father was walking away into the water. The coffin stuck in the sand like an abandoned boat in some painter's vision of a lighthouse scene. Her father wasn't alone. There were hundreds—thousands—of other people walking into the water. The surf grew rougher still and storm clouds filled the sky. Thunder and lightning rolled out from inside of them and lightning slashed away the darkness in a frenzied brush stroke. More lightning…

…and then nothing. White.

Dawn is standing in a field of flowers—the same flowers from her father's wake—she's pregnant and rubbing her swollen belly in what can only be described as bliss. Her mother is smiling at her. The father is nowhere to be found, but it doesn't matter, the best thing he can offer her is to leave and have no hand in raising the child. More storm clouds. The thunder and lightning return.

She's driving. It's raining. The sky is bleeding purple and red. The car is swerving. She can't see. It's spinning. She's screaming. There's an impact. She smacks her head and her vision goes black as lighting strikes across her eyes.

She awakes and knows something is wrong. She's back at the beach, staring at her father who is now standing knee deep in the ocean holding a baby—her baby. She feels her stomach, but it feels hollow with only the faintest trace of a ghost.

She walks toward the water but with each step the ocean recedes. She tries to run to it, to feel the water swallow her feet, but despite her best attempts the ocean is no closer. A message in a bottle is at her feet and it's a suicide note from her mother that goes on seemingly forever. She drank herself to death, and the bottle in Dawn's hands was the very bottle she was found clutching, empty of everything but regrets. The regrets were hastily jotted down on the note.

Lightning.

She hits her head against the window and wakes up. For a minute she's not sure where she is but hopes she's still pregnant and is able to stop the car from spinning out of control but then she looks over and sees Jon-Jon and knows that the damage is done and the dream is over.

"Hey sleepy-head. Feel refreshed?"

"Uh…not at all. My neck is killing me. How long was I out?"

"I dunno, maybe like an hour, hour and a half."

"Damn. Are we there yet?"

"Not you too. It's bad enough I have to hear it from these dicks in the back and now you?"

"Relax."

In the back of the van Chung-Hee sat squished next to Chuck. They were both fairly small men, but with so many people in so little space everywhere was tight. He leaned away from him as best he could but with every bounce on the road he just ended up bouncing right back into him.

When the van grew silent—as it often did—Chung-Hee's mind drifted to thoughts of Naraka. This was far from what he imagined the underworld to be, but what this was certainly wasn't the world he remembered. Naraka is a place where the souls of the sinful are sent for expiation of sins. For redemption—reconciliation, even forgiveness. Chung-Hee could think of nothing in his life that would secure him such a fate. He was never able to live up to his parent's expectations, true, but neither was he the bane of their existence. From what he could tell he was a hard-working man, more so than his peers. Everything he owned he worked for. He was given nothing in this life other than the necessities he needed, the love he warranted, and the expectations to live up to—or at least strive for.

Naraka is supposed to be a place of justice. Not a place like this— a place of torment, of suffering unwarranted. Chung-Hee considered the possibility that he was dead. He was dead and unaware of his demise or sins and as he came closer to righting his wrongs a sense of clarity would overcome him. And if that were the case then he could think of nothing he did that would lead him toward any sort of reconciliation. He was simply trying to survive—as were the rest of the people in his group.

How he could atone for a sin he didn't know he committed was beyond him. All he could do was what he thought was right, which is what he's been doing all along. In his mind, Naraka was a terrible place full of terrible people having unthinkable things being done to them for the sake of penance. He envisioned people being boiled, skinned, beaten, raped, and even eaten. Naraka was a land that was ruled by darkness to bring about light, full of evil, vile, punishments for those that deserved such a fate. It was no place for children—what could they have done? And yet, they were here too.

Chung-Hee shook it from his mind, though he knew he would eventually drift there again. Naraka was a place for the dead and for the wicked—not a place for him, and not a place for the people he had come to travel with. They were good people—he was a good person—Naraka was not for them.

He opened his eyes and watched the world go by as they drove down the road. Every now and again he would catch a glimpse of one the lumbering dead that stumbled about in search of flesh. What sins did they make, he wondered. What did they do that deserved their unnatural return from oblivion?

Chuck stared straight ahead, but he wasn't looking at anything. He was deep in thought about nothing. He was thinking of the beach. The sand between his toes, the sea breeze rustling his hair, and the women. Good golly Miss Molly was he thinking about those Florida women. The Beach Boys always seemed to favor the California women, and Chuck couldn't fault them, they were just fine as well, but for Chuck, the women back home were the only women for him. Sanibel, Bonita Springs, and Marco Island were some of his favorite places to visit and even further north at Cedar Key would be great this time of year. Most of the college kids and hipsters would be heading out to Key West, or—God forbid—Miami, but there were plenty of places in Florida that suited Chuck just fine. Full of the slow-paced, relaxing qualities that kept him down south for so long.

Marco Island was full of great times just a few months ago. He fell in lust with a freckle-faced woman name Maggie. She had an old lady's name, but a college girl's face and a tennis player's body. Her hair was auburn and seemed to radiate in the sun. They spent a lot of time together and ended it amicably, though Chuck would often think of her. He wondered why they quit each other so quick and tried not to think of it. It was fun while it lasted, and he hoped she was safe. He thought of being there now, sitting outside on her deck looking out on the water. He could taste the fresh Cubano sandwiches she loved to make and the Mango Mamma wine they loved to wash it down with.

Luckily for Chuck, before the thoughts had time to depress him,

Joseph hollered from behind him, "We there yet?"

"It's getting really fucking old, man."

There were a few chuckles, and then the sounds of introspection.

12 IMPULSES

Jim had packed the few belongings he cared about enough to lug around and the clothes he knew he'd get the most wear out of as well as all of his socks and underwear. He wished he was going on vacation, but knew that it would be anything but. Regardless he needed to get the hell out of his home. He was developing a nasty case of cabin fever and if he didn't take this chance to get out now he knew he would end up running out of the house screaming nonsense in the buff. He might drive himself insane enough to run into the loving embrace of one of the dead.

He crept over to Sarah after putting his bags next to the door downstairs. She looked so peaceful. The little bit of sleep she was getting had already managed to soften the hard lines that only moments ago were etched into her face. She was attractive, and the longer he looked at her sleeping form, the more he realized this. He lingered, and his mind ran through some deviant ideas. His heart raced. She moaned in her sleep, and shifted. Jim decided to turn away and walk out as briskly as he could. He returned to his room and stared out the window.

Sarah continued sleeping, and Jim knew he should've woken her but the little nasty fantasies brewing in his mind had the very good possibility of becoming reality.

He looked out the window and the few dead things that roamed seemingly aimlessly about the streets soon staggered out of view, and for a moment things looked normal, but then a staggering ghoul moved into view once again.

He stretched out across the bed, eyeing the doorway, picturing Sarah walking in and taking her clothes off. Straddling him. His hand found its way down his pants and he urgently wanted to run into the other room and show her what it found.

***

Laura fell asleep in his lap in the rocking chair, and despite his body's every ache and his mind's general good sense to not further hurt himself Walter carried her to the bed and tucked her in. He filled another few fingers of brandy and left the love of his life to sleep soundly. He gently closed the door and joined his children downstairs.

"What's the occasion, dad?"

"Can't an old man have a drink without everyone raising an eyebrow?"

"If you can't have a drink now, then when can you?"

"Exactly. Now, what have I missed?"

"Well, we were thinking maybe it was time to start searching through our neighbors homes for supplies."

"Nonsense. We have plenty here."

"Actually, Walter, we don't. Considering how many of us there are we'll go through supplies much quicker than we thought."

"When are you going to call me dad? When I'm dead?"

"Sorry, dad."

"Did you count everything up?"

"The tally is right here," she handed him the notebook.

"I trust ya."

"We might as well do it now before we get surrounded by these things. The longer we wait the worse we're going to make it on ourselves and let's face it, no one is coming back to there homes any time soon…if ever…"

"Fine, you kids are old enough to make up your own minds. What can I do?"

"I don't know, I figured me and Barb could go into the homes. You're more than welcome to join us. Maria is going to stay here. Honestly, we really haven't thought it out much."

"We just know we should do it, and there's no sense in waiting."

"Who knows what could happen in the next few days, right now they are spread out far enough that we can maneuver through them, take care of the close ones, get what we can and get back home."

"All right. Can we at least wait till daybreak before we do this?"

"Of course. We weren't just going to go and do it now."

"Well how am I supposed to know? You all look ready to go."

"Just trying to be ready, dad. You don't want us sitting around in our pajamas do you?"

"No, not at all."

"Why don't you go sit down and enjoy your brandy?"

"Only if one of you will join me."

"I'll go get a bottle of wine," Maria said, smiling.

"Two glasses...please?" Barb said, holding out two fingers like a peace sign.

Maria went into the kitchen, fetching a bottle of Pinot Noir from the wine rack her father-in-law built. There were several bottles left— not nearly enough—and mostly just bottles of Pinot Noir. In the cupboard next to the rack were the wine glasses and Maria almost dropped one while she reached on tiptoes to get them.

She returned to the living room, uncorked the bottle of wine and poured herself and Barbara a full glass each of the deep red fluid.

They sat down on the couch with Jeff. Walter sat in his chair. The room was quiet and dark.

"So, what shall we drink to?" Walter asked.

"Being alive."

"A better tomorrow."

"How about world peace?"

"The ladies got it right. Maybe you should be taking some notes. Here's to being alive and for a better tomorrow." Walter raised his drink. Maria and Barbara did the same; Jeff reached for the bottle of wine. Then they all took a swig of their fluids and began to talk about looting their neighbors homes for supplies.

***

Carrie was just one of the most unlikeable people on earth, and must have been before the world went to hell. It was in her body language and in her expressions, probably more so than in her words, but it oozed from her. Alexis was certain that was the main reason she was still alive—that and even the deaders probably didn't want her as one of their own. She probably would taste sour to them.

Alexis wanted to pull her hair out. The kids were growing restless and bored. Chris, the youngest, in particular was having a hard time sitting still. He was climbing and squirming over the others, which in turn bothered them and made them squirm.

It had gotten to the point where they were starting to hit each other. Alexis was quite simply out of her area of expertise. She was growing short with them, losing her patience, and she could tell Carrie was ready to snap. If that happened Alexis was ready to go off on her but she really didn't want to. She knew it was just the mounting frustration.

Gerty would've known how to handle them. Alexis was barely out of her teens, just having turned twenty in the spring, and she had no siblings.

Yussef played with Nick, passing Hot Wheels back and forth and riding them along the seats and headrests.

Then Chris started crying for chocolate milk.

Abdul-Ba'ith had to have felt the tension building in the car, and was probably feeling the stress as well because he finally spoke after at least an hour of silence. The only reason he spoke before was because Alexis was trying to make conversation. "I'm going to signal to the others that we need to pull over."

"Why what's wrong?" Carrie looked nervously about the vehicle.

"We need a break. The kids need to get some air. We all need to get some air. And we should stretch—my leg is cramping."

"We should dump these kids out and keep going," she said coldly.

Abdul-Ba'ith pushed down on the horn and put his hazards on. Once he saw the break lights in front of him he began to pull over to the side of the road.

Scott jumped out of the car and jogged over to Abdul-Ba'ith as he stepped out of the truck. "Everything okay?"

"Yes. We just needed to take a break…the kids are growing restless."

"Fine with me. I gotta take a leak anyway. I'll go tell the others."

"Thank you."

Carrie stepped out and began stretching. Alexis ushered the kids over to the side of the road and had them stretch as well. Most of them decided to horse around, but at least they were moving around and getting out some of that energy.

"Does anybody have to go to the bathroom?"

They all did.

"Oh, okay…"

Leela cupped her hands over her crotch and began to jump up and down, "I gotta go!"

"Okay, Leela. Girls! Come on, follow me over this way and we'll go."

Leela followed urgently. Stacey slowly moved in pursuit, clutching a filthy lion Beanie Baby named Roar, which her father brought home for her one day after work.

"Abdul, can you have the boys go?"

He looked at her, his rigid eyebrows curling up and his eyes widening in uncertainty.

"But I…I, oh man, okay."

Abdul never had any children of his own and in his family many of the men were very hands off with their children. He looked at the boys. To him they looked old enough to know what to do and hoped he was right. He looked to Carrie for support but she just looked at him and said, "Not me, I hate kids."

He shrugged his shoulders, "Boys. You have to urinate?"

Yussef turned to him and nodded, Chris did too. Nick looked at the ground away from everyone.

"Well, then spread out and go. You know how to go right? You're big boys now, yes?"

"Yes."

"Uh-huh."

"Good, go." Abdul-Ba'ith breathed a sigh of relief, then noticed that Nick had not moved from his spot. Maybe he was bashful, he figured.

He moved over to him, kneeling down and putting his hand to his shoulder. "You're Nick, right?"

The boy nodded.

"How old are you Nick?"

"Five."

"Then you don't need help, right? You can go like the other boys. Just walk over there and do it in the grass. No one will look."

"I…I…"

"Are you afraid?"

"No…"

"It's okay if you are. I know it's scary now."

"It's not that."

"Then what?"

"I already went." Nick said, as he pointed to his wet pants.

"Oh. Well, uh… I don't know what to tell you. Do you have any more in there?"

Nick nodded.

"Then get the rest out and I will tell Alexis. I'm sure we can find you something to wear. Next time, just tell me you have to go, and I will stop the truck, okay?"

Nick nodded again and then ran off to finish the job.

Abdul-Ba'ith rubbed his temples. Dealing with the living dead was easy—kids were the real challenge.

13 LEFT BEHIND

Hours had passed before Sarah had woken up. She felt groggy and disoriented. She had to look about the room before she remembered where she was. Her eyes found the clock and after realizing how much time had passed she grew both agitated with Jim and thankful because she was able to rest. The extra sleep made her feel a million times more human.

She got up and walked out of the room almost stumbling into Jim, "Oh, hey. Thanks for letting me sleep, but I guess we should get going, huh?"

"Yeah, I'm all packed and ready to go. I heard you stirring so I figured I'd come and see if you're ready."

"Good to go."

"I'm really nervous. I haven't had to deal with them much close up."

"You'll be fine. Just move quickly and don't let them grab you."

"Grab?"

"They won't let go and once they get a hand on you, their teeth will be next."

"Now I'm not nervous at all," he paused, thinking about pushing her into the room and closing the door. "I uh...my car is packed up. I didn't have much water, but I just about filled the trunk with all the food and drinks I do have. Suitcase and backpack in the back seat."

"Do you have any weapons?"

"Not really. I have a shovel and an old baseball bat that I had to use a few times."

"That'll do. Are they inside?"

"Yup. In the garage."

"Perfect," she said, heading for the stairs, "let's go."

He followed, picturing himself grabbing her by the neck and pulling her back.

The garage was dark but enough light came from underneath the bottom of the garage door to highlight most of the objects in the small space. She moved swiftly to the passenger's side as Jim grabbed the shovel and bat from near the door. After shoving them in the backseat he hopped behind the wheel.

"Ready?" He asked, nervousness pouring from his voice and evident in his shaking hands and sweaty forehead.

"I am, are you?"

"No. But let's do it, right?"

"Right."

Jim pushed the open button on the garage door remote and watched intently as light flooded the room.

"Fuck, I'm scared."

"Me too."

The garage door seemed to open so slowly. They could see a pair of legs staggering forward—a simple silhouette against the pale yellow daylight. By the time the door opened the dead thing stumbled inside. Jim drove forward, knocking the dead thing back. The thump of its dead body on the car startled Jim terribly.

"Go!"

Jim gassed the car and hit the close button on the remote, dropping it afterwards.

"Fuck, fuck, fuck, which way?"

"You said you knew where you were going!"

"I do, I'm sorry, just…fuck!" Jim was almost hyperventilating.

"Just drive. Breath. And drive. Just start moving away… now."

"Okay, okay," Jim said as he pulled out of the driveway and into the road.

The garage door closed and the dead thing got to its feet, staggering after them.

Jim drove through town toward the school. He was trying to keep his breathing under control but so far hadn't been successful. Sarah just sat back and kept her eyes on their surroundings. She took note of how run down everything looked now that no one was taking care of their lawn or sweeping the streets. Lawns were being overrun by weeds and once proud landscapes were now nothing more than tall grasses and specimen plants aching for pruning and shearing. Sarah realized how quickly everything falls apart when no one is tending to it.

Jim swerved nearly hitting a deader that was stumbling down the road. He wanted to yell at the thing. To tell it to get the hell out of the road, but it would've been useless.

A few more deaders were in the distance—nothing more than shadows wearing shredded clothes and dragging swollen feet along the warming asphalt. The sun glistening behind the dead things—a big warm ball of hope that made everything seem normal with its presence. But this was anything but. This was certainly something new under the sun.

They rounded the corner and Sarah could see the school in the distance. The sun glinting off the flagpole, and the aluminum flashing around the edge of the roof. But where was the sun glinting off the cars and trucks that formed the convoy? There was only one truck left—a simple box truck. Where were the others? Sarah's mind reeled and her stomach felt sick.

They left.

They left her.

"No…"

"What? This is the school you meant, right?"

"Yeah, this is the school, but they left. They fucking left me!"

Jim didn't know what to say. He continued to drive.

"They left me for dead."

"Maybe they thought you were dead."

As they came upon the school she could see she was wrong. There was another car that had been blocked by the truck. They pulled over to it.

"Holy shit."

"Oh, God…oh, my god." Sarah cried.

Inside the car was a dead little girl reaching her hands through the driver's side window in a futile attempt to get out. She was pale, but aside from her complexion, the bullet in her throat and the dried blood that covered her body she looked alive. Sarah recognized her. She couldn't remember the kid's name, but she knew her face. She stared into the kid's eyes and cried.

"Go."

"Go where?"

"Just go back to your place."

"What about her?"

"Do you want to go put her out of her misery?"

"I…no, no I don't want to do that."

"Then just go, if we had a gun I would put her down, but I don't. So just go already, okay?"

With that, he drove away.

Sarah didn't have to turn around to see the lifeless little girl staring through the grimy glass.

"Do you want to try and catch up with your group?"

"We'd just get lost. We'll never find them. They could be hours away by now. We're better off just laying low at your place till we can think of something better."

"Okay, yeah, sure."

"Are you okay with that?"

"Yeah, it's been working out just fine for me. I was just excited to hook up and get the hell out of here you know?"

"I can imagine. I'd probably've lost my mind had I been stuck at home alone through all this."

Jim remained silent as the bad thoughts invaded his mind again. He'd never acted on any of his darker impulses before, but the reasons not too seemed nonexistent at the moment.

They arrived back at Jim's house without incident and managed to get inside without drawing too much attention. The street was empty of deaders and the last few they drove past were too far away to follow them with any sort of precision, though they had no problem figuring out where people were. Sarah would say they were drawn to people—some sort of instinct.

"Think we should leave the food and stuff in the car?"

"Yeah, never know when we might need to get out in a hurry."

"That's smart."

Sarah opened the door and entered the home, "We should check the window."

"Go ahead. I'm right behind you."

14 MASHED BRAINS

Scrrrtttttch. Scrrrtttttch. Scrrrtttttch.

A police officer in a filthy blue uniform dragged his shredded leg along the street. His uniform sported many a tears that framed bite marks and gouged flesh. His leg was mostly bone and thin slivers of muscle tissue with the frayed ends of veins dangling with each step.

Scrrrtttttch. Scrrrtttttch. Scrrrtttttch.

The soles of his dress blacks looked chewed as well, but it was simply the wear and tear from dragging along the blacktop. He walked with a hunch, as if he could fall over at any moment and his left hand twitched erratically. His right hand was missing most of its digits and at a distance it looked like a red stump.

Scrrrtttttch. Scrrrtttttch. Scrrrtttttch.

His face was mostly intact aside from a large chunk of meat missing from his cheek and jaw line. It looked like a bear could've just taken one swat and ripped it right off. His pallor was waning to a steely gray color like the tie clip that still held his dark blue blood covered tie in place.

Scrrrtttttch. Scrrrtttttch. Scrrrtttttch.

"What's that noise?"

"Heads up. Sounds like a deader around.

Scrrrtttttch. Scrrrtttttch.

"I think I see 'em."

"Scott! Right there."

"Oh, shit. I got it."

Scott retrieved a crowbar from the car and jogged over to it as it shambled closer.

Scrrrttttch. Scrrrttttch. Scrrrttttch.

He swung the crowbar over his head and down onto the shoulder of the deader. The man in blue went hard to the ground. His ravaged leg giving way immediately to the blow. The dead thing continued to crawl forward as if it meant to drop to the ground and nearly grabbed Scott by the foot as he smashed the crowbar down on the deader's head.

A wet cracking noise filled the air as Scott brought the bar back up to swing again. Another hit and a hole formed in the back of the dead man's head. Gooey blood and a lump of mashed brain oozed out of the hole and onto the street.

Scott pushed the dead thing with the crowbar. Aside from its twitching it seemed to be dead again.

"I think we should wrap up our little break and get back on the road. Agreed?"

"Yeah, let's get the fuck out of here."

As everyone dispersed to their vehicles more of the shambling dead appeared from off the road and out of the catacombs of vehicles that clogged the roads.

"Looks like we started moving just in time," Frankie pointed out, almost unemotionally.

"Holy shit," Eddie said, "Let's move! There's a bunch more."

Alexis hurried the kids to the car, Carrie ran past them, knocking Stacey to the ground and jumped into the passenger's side without so much as a care. Abdul stood in the street waiting for the kids to get in before he started the truck. When he soon did, he gave Carrie the look of death. His patience with her was starting to wane. She seemed unimpressed.

Janice looked out the window, wishing she'd been outside and within reach of the terrible dead things. She closed her eyes, almost wincing from the guilt she felt from the thought. She didn't want to feel this way—she didn't want die, but she knew she couldn't really live anymore.

Joseph saw the look on her face. Figuring she was simply upset at the sight of the dead things he put her arm around her and tried to comfort her.

"It's okay mom. They can't get us. We're moving."

"I know, honey, I know…"

But she wanted them to touch her. She wanted them to pull her down and rip her to shreds so she could feel what the broken pieces of her family felt and so that she could be with them again.

Jon-Jon pushed the pedal down hard and started to make up for the time lost pissing and bitching on the side of the road.

The dead things disappeared in the dust kicked up by spinning tires.

The dead man in blue continued to twitch, like a car in the dead of winter failing to start.

15 OLD MAN MOMENT

A fuzzy orange sun started to rise up above the horizon. The sky looked like a set of melted crayons, streaky hot wax being pulled and pushed into a pleasing morning light.

Walter sat on the stoop, drinking water from a coffee cup, and staring at the dead things shambling around.

Where were they going? Why did they want to eat us? Why are they here? What have we done?

No one answered his questions and the dead began to notice him, shifting on stiff legs to change their direction.

"Yeah, come on over boys. I still got plenty of fight left in me," Walter said, putting down his glass and reaching for the bat.

He began walking toward them, hunched over like a predator, bat held off to the side ready to strike. His knees clicked as he walked. His neck grew tight. He cursed his aging body.

The dead thing was in reach.

Walter swung the bat. It connected with the dead things neck and sent it reeling off to the side, but it didn't fall. Before it could steady itself Walter struck the dead thing again. This time it went down.

A few other deaders began to shamble closer.

Walter put his foot on the throat of the dead thing, pinning it to the ground. Its dead fingers wrapped around his foot. It was trying to pull his foot closer to its dead, dry mouth.

"What do you want from us?"

It gave no answer.

"Is there anyone home in there?" Walter asked, tapping the bat on the dead things head.

Still, no answer.

The other deaders were getting closer, but Walter couldn't take his eyes off the one under his foot. He was studying it. Searching for something in its eyes, but there was nothing to find.

There was no shred of humanity. No emotion. Nothing. Just reanimated flesh. Lifeless limbs that mimicked man, a puppeteer's creation come alive with no use for its strings and all fluidity lost.

"Dad! What the hell are you doing?"

Walter took the bat, raising it above his head and brought it down full force into the top of the dead things head. It's head exploded from the impact and black blood spattered up Walter's pant legs.

"Just talking to the neighbors, sweetheart. You have the rifle?"

"Of course I do."

"Well what are you waiting for? I could use a hand."

"You come out here like this by yourself again and I'll shoot you."

"Promise?"

"Promise."

"Atta girl."

Barbara took aim and fired. She hit one in the stomach. Another shot and she missed. Walter took down another.

The shots brought Jeff and Maria to the door. Jeff grabbed a spade shovel and ran to his father's side. Maria watched in admiration as Barbara held the rifle and took aim at the deaders. She took a deep breath and squeezed the trigger. The kickback rocked her entire frame. The bullet tore through the throat of one of the dead things. Jeff finished it off.

They stood among the scattering of dead again twitching bodies.

"What were you thinking doing this by yourself?"

"I wasn't. I was having one of my old man moments, okay. Just leave it."

"Fine, but you know it was stupid, right?"

"Leave it."

"Fine."

"So, I'm thinking…maybe we should start burning these things. We're asking for disease if we just leave them here."

"Agreed, but that's going to be disgusting. Do you think the fire would draw more of them here?"

"No more than the rifle will, I'd think."

"Can it wait till we're done scavenging?"

"Sure can. Will do it tomorrow. Since we're all up, maybe we should get started with that, eh?"

"Guess we should. Also, I want to get the kids outside for a little bit."

"I've been thinking about that too."

"How so?"

"Well, I think Davis had a good idea about walling off the town. Maybe he was thinking too big too soon. I don't know, but what I do know is that we can fence off the house. It'd give us a buffer; make things harder for the deaders for sure. And it would allow us to take the kids outside without having to worry so much. I know they need it—hell we all need it. They're getting cooped up and running amuck inside."

"Tell me about it."

"I will. But first things first, let's get what supplies we can today. Burn these things up tomorrow and see what we can do about fencing off the house the day after."

"Sounds good. You going to come with us?"

"Might as well."

Maria hadn't noticed, but Tommy had come to the door. He was standing just behind her with the look of shock on his face. As Jeff and Walter made their way back to the house they saw him, and both hoped he had not witnessed any of the violence.

"Tommy, what are you doing out here?"

Maria turned around gasping. "Honey, what are you doing out here?"

Laura came running to the door, "There you are! Tommy." She knew the boy had seen something he shouldn't have. She felt the need to explain, "We were playing Hide and Seek. Tommy should've been hiding, but I...I guess he came out here. I'm so sorry. Did he...?"

"It's not your fault, ma."

"Tommy, did you see anything?"

"Are those people dead?" He pointed to the bodies scattered around the lawn.

Maria wrapped him up in his arms.

"Yes, Tommy," Jeff said. "Those people are dead. There is something wrong with them...something made them turn into bad people—into monsters—they want to hurt us, so we had to stop them."

"M-monsters?"

"Yup…it's sort of like that comic you like, Mutant Man. The one where he fights zombies."

"Those people are zombies?"

"They were."

"But the ones in Mutant Man are from space, and they're green. These look like people. Like dead people."

Maria held him tighter, her tears running down his cheek as well as her own.

"We didn't want you to see this, Tommy. This is why we don't come outside much, and why there's no school. Something happened, and now zombies are real. They're not green monsters from space with glowing eyes, they don't run or fly, but they're still monsters, and we have to be the good guys."

"Like Mutant Man?"

"Yup, just like Mutant Man, but we don't have any special powers. Are you okay, now?"

"I guess. I don't like seeing them, dad. The dead people like that. It's scary."

"I know. I know it is. Me and grandpa are going to take care of it okay?"

"Okay," Tommy said.

"Now why don't you go back inside with grandma and play with Wally and Sandra?"

"Okay, dad."

Maria kissed him on the forehead and he ran inside with Laura.

Walter patted his son on the shoulder, "We couldn't keep it from them forever. Sooner or later they'd have to see one. It's better this way. At least he didn't see one of them up close and trying to eat him."

"That would certainly scar him for life. I just hope he didn't see us bashing them."

"I don't think he did. He just seemed freaked out about all the bodies. If either of us walked out thinking everything was honky-dory and saw all these bodies we'd get pretty freaked out too."

Jeff nodded. He knew he wouldn't be able to shelter his kids from the dead outside forever. Part of him felt relieved. Another part wanted to bring Sandra and Wally outside and let them have a look so it would all be done and over with, but he decided not too.

"Okay, Maria, I think you should head inside and lock everything up. Barb, you set to go?"

"As much as I'll ever be."

"Then let's get this over with," Walter huffed.

16 OFF-ROADING

"Well, we were doing good for awhile." Jon-Jon said, staring at the clogged road just up ahead.

"Damn," said Eddie as he sat perched over Jon's shoulder.

"I knew it wouldn't last."

"Think we could take this van off-roading?"

"That's about our only option if we want to stay in our vehicles, I think, but look how steep it is."

"Think we'll tip?"

"Fucked if I know."

"Wanna get out and check it out?"

"Nope, but I will."

"Let's do it."

Most of the usual suspects got out of their vehicles when they saw Jon-Jon and Eddie head out of the van and to the side of the road. The road was thick with vehicles. Many had bumped into each other, others looked as if they had tried driving other vehicles off the road. It was a small taste of what the chaos was like on the first days.

"Let's keep some distance between us okay?"

"Yeah, it's really tight so everybody maintain some breathing room incase we need to move back in a hurry."

"I'll climb up this truck and be the eyes in the sky," Chung-Hee said, hopping into the bed of a pick up truck and then onto its cab.

Eddie stood on the edge of the road looking off, "Damn. It is really steep. And looks like a few folks gave it a shot before rolling over."

Jon-Jon surveyed the area and took in the vehicles that had ventured off road. They indeed rolled due to the incline, but maybe they were going to fast or turning to sharply he thought for a moment.

"Maybe if we drove down straight and into that gulley." Frankie pointed out.

"Yeah, the brush doesn't look to thick over there and the land levels out a bit. Then we might be able to follow it through and bypass the congestion."

"Let's just hope we can get back on the road at some point."

"So long as we keep moving forward we should be able to."

"Hey guys," Chung-Hee yelled, "we got company."

Scott jogged over to Chung-Hee and hopped up onto the truck with him. "Shit. We got a lot of company!"

Judy ran over to her husband. Concern, worry, and fear all blended together into one expression across her plain, yet attractive, face.

"We need to move!"

"Where are they coming from?" Frankie yelled out.

"They're coming from the brush on the other side. A few dozen of them. Too many for us to take on."

"Jon, can you lead us down there?"

"What choice do we have? We're going to have to back up a touch to get around these cars to get over there," Jon-Jon said as they began to hurry back toward the vehicles.

"Hey, Abdul, you're gonna have to back up and lead us around, okay?"

"Sure."

"Let's go! Let's go!" Jon-Jon yelled.

Scott and Chung-Hee jumped down, racing back to their vehicles. Judy grabbed Scott's hand and pulled him to a run.

Abdul spun his truck around. The dead were mere yards away and could be seen as clear as day on the road now. He drove closer to them causing Carrie to scream at him. If she weren't so annoying he'd have enjoyed her growing anxiety. He turned the truck sharply and headed over to the side of the road. A small sedan was in the way of an otherwise relatively clear path to the other side.

"Hold on tight."

"You're not going--"

Abdul slammed on the gas and sped forward, hitting the sedan hard enough and at such an angle that is pushed the car to the side and only cost them a bumpy ride and a headlight.

"You're fucking crazy," Carrie screamed, "you almost gave me a heart attack!"

"Would you rather a heart attack, or having your skin ripped off by those things we just passed? Well?"

He took the truck down the side of the road. The incline was steep and the truck went down fast. The ride was bumpy and Carrie bitched and moaned the entire way down. Abdul hit his head on the ceiling at one point and as they reached the bottom he almost steered into a tree.

Scott and Judy were right behind them, bumping up and down just as much. Abdul moved his truck away just in time as Scott and Judy began to fish tail right into them. They hit the tree that Abdul almost had, but only barely.

Jon-Jon held the van at the top of the road till Scott turned the vehicle the right way around and followed Abdul through the level patch of land. The dead were clawing at the back of the van now and moving up its sides.

"Go! Go now!" Dawn screamed, as she stared at them through the rearview mirror.

"All right, all right!"

Jon-Jon gave the van just enough gas to start down the slope and once the van was on it, it bounced quickly and violently down.

"Hold on tight!"

The van dipped so hard forward from one of the bumps near the bottom that the front bumper caught and dug into the earth, crunching under the weight of the van as it tipped end of over end, landing on its roof and partially crashing into the tree that Scott had barely hit, crushing the rear doors rendering them useless.

The dead shambled slowly down the hill as the sounds of panicked screaming continued inside the van.

17 RAIDERS

Walter, Jeff, and Barbara headed over to the neighbors house. Walter drove the pick up truck to the closest neighbor. Walter didn't particularly care for these neighbors. The man was an ass who treated his wife like shit. He always seemed to be arguing with her about something stupid. Walter once made it clear to him that if he ever hit her he'd have to argue with her through a wired jaw.

The truck came to a stop and Walter stepped out. He took the baseball bat from the bed of the truck, and grabbed the shovel, tossing it to Jeff as he got out. Barbara stepped out with rifle in hand. Walter wanted her to take the back and use the rifle if needed. He was certain him and Jeff could handle any deaders on their own with the melee weapons, but just in case, having Barbara with the rifle wasn't a bad idea—especially since she was shaping up to be a decent shot.

Walter led his children up the steps. He peered in to the front window, and though it was bright outside it seemed no light found it's way in the home. It was dark and grey, like everything had a thick layer of dust on it. He imagined they must have drawn the shades, locked the windows and the doors and as he tried to the doorknob he knew he was right. It was locked, as was the window.

"We're going to have to break in."

"I'll do it. Step back."

Jeff eyed the door and hoped his idea worked. He rammed the head of the spade shovel into the doorjamb where the lock was. The wood splintered and his arms vibrated as he struck the lock. He rammed it a few more times and was then able to pry open the door.

Walter looked around the yard for deaders. Seeing nothing he led them inside the dark house.

Jeff's heart pounded. He tried to listen for anything in the house, but he was unable to hear anything over his own breathing and racing heartbeat.

"Come on," Walter said. "Let's be quick about this."

Walter walked through the home cautiously but still swiftly. Checking each room as he moved through it. They found the kitchen and Walter rummaged through the cabinets till he found a box of trash bags. There was also a flashlight in there that he grabbed and put in his back pocket.

"Here," he ripped open the box and handed each of them a bag, "fill it up with supplies and run it to the truck."

Barbara slung the rifle over her shoulder and loaded the bag efficiently. She opened the cabinets and began throwing in boxes of pasta, canned goods, spices, and your run of the mill non-perishables.

Jeff opened the freezer and was hit in the face with the smell of spoiled meat. He quickly closed it and opened the fridge for the same scent, but grabbed two bottles of soda and a small pack of bottled water.

Walter opened the pantry and bagged everything he could. He grabbed cleaning items as well as food and stuffed the bags till they were ripping from the weight.

"Okay, let's run these back to the truck. Let's go."

They dumped the bags into the bed of the truck, taking in their surroundings the whole time. Walter's head moved from side to side and he kept looking back to their home to make sure no deaders had gone in search of living flesh.

"Going back," Jeff said, as he bounded the steps.

They hit the kitchen one more time and were only able to scrape together another bag. Walter found a bathroom on the same floor and grabbed everything out of the medicine cabinet save for the used toothbrushes. He added the items to the bag and set it by the door.

They continued on the level and while opening what Walter suspected was a closet door they stumbled upon the basement. Walter grabbed the flashlight from his back pocket and descended.

"Wait here till I give the all clear," he said midway down the staircase.

Walter reached the bottom and spun the light around the room. It was a small damp basement. In one corner sat a workbench, in the other a washer and dryer set with a slop sink. On one side of the basement was a line of Rubbermaid storage cabinets.

"Is it clear?"

"Yeah, yeah, come on down. Bring the bags."

They opened the storage cabinets and emptied what little was in there. Jeff grabbed a case of water and they headed back up stairs.

They went through the rest of the house and found little else aside from some health aids in the upstairs bathroom and linen closet.

After loading up the truck they moved on to the next house, and then the next. Walter felt a growing anxiety in his stomach the further away their home looked in the rearview mirror, but at least when they got back they would be better equipped to whether the storm.

18 HOLD ON

Alexis watched in terror, staring out the back window as the van tipped over.

"Oh, my God! Abdul, we have to do something!"

Chris started crying and Stacey yelled at him to shut up.

"Stay here with the children. Carrie, be ready to drive away if need be. I'll do what I can."

"How about I drive away now?"

Abdul grabbed a tire-iron, "Enough, Carrie, or so help me I will use this on you when I get back," he yelled, then hurried over to the van. Scott and Judy followed behind, each brandishing a similar melee weapon.

The dead shambled slowly down the hill. Some toppled over and rolled down the hill. It would be comical if they were removed from the reality of the situation.

Inside the van Eddie bled profusely from his nose. He opened the side door and started helping everyone out. Jon-Jon and Dawn were both unconscious in the front, and Eddie feared one if not both were dead. Frankie crawled out of the van, dizzy and disoriented. Abdul ran over to him and pointed him toward his truck.

"Go!" He yelled, but Frankie stood there, hoping he could be of help.

Chuck, and Chung-Hee were next out of the van.

The dead were now approaching.

Scott went on the offensive and attacked the closest one, cracking its head open on the first swing and sending it reeling backwards.

Eddie stepped out of the van, pulling his mother out. Janice clutched her head and a thin sliver of crimson ran down her face. Joseph followed, looking only frazzled and angry.

Abdul opened the passenger side door and shook Dawn to consciousness. She was disoriented and her vision was blurry. She began to scream and smack Abdul away. He calmed her down, reassuring her that he wasn't going to hurt her as the sounds of the dead began to buzz in his ears like a swarm of flies around road kill.

Scott took down another. Then Judy took one down. Frankie attacked another. Yet still more came and Dawn was just getting out of the van.

"What the hell is taking so long?" Carrie whined.

"It looks like some of them are hurt," Alexis replied.

"Hurt bad? Should we go?"

"I want to go," Nick pleaded.

"We have to wait," Stacey told him.

"We're not going anywhere," Alexis yelled.

Alexis continued to look out the window. Eddie was walking his mother to the other car. She couldn't see Joseph, and hoped he wasn't hurt.

Judy was checking Jon-Jon for a pulse. A surge of relief washed over her when she found one. He wasn't waking up and she couldn't lift him by herself. She looked around and Joseph met her eyes. He ran over instinctively and she yelled for him to hurry.

"He's alive!"

"Thank Christ," Joseph replied. "Let's get him out of there."

Joseph was a strong young guy and had no trouble pulling Jon-Jon out of the van and hoisting him over his shoulder.

"Follow me," Judy said as she started jogging away.

"Everyone's out of the van." Abdul said, pulling Frankie back from the onslaught of dead.

"Let's go!" Abdul yelled.

Scott turned and ran, surveying the area for his wife.

They converged at the two vehicles, the dead not far behind.

"Fuck! We're not all gonna fit."

Abdul looked at his truck. "Guys, get on top of the truck. Hold on to the roof racks."

"They can't ride up there!" Carrie yelled.

"Joe, put Jon in our truck. Janice, get in there too. Dawn I think you should hop in too, and if anyone else can fit. Chung you might be able to squeeze in the back on top of the luggage."

"The rest of you start climbing," Scott said as he hopped in the driver's seat.

Eddie and his brother Joseph climbed up Scott's SUV, laid down on their bellies, holding tight to the roof racks. Chung-Hee hopped inside the SUV and sat on top of the luggage in the back, while Chuck and Frankie climbed up on top of Abdul's SUV.

Frankie slapped the roof to signal they were good to go and Abdul began to accelerate and not a moment too soon, since the dead were already in reach of the truck behind them.

The dead clawed at the window as Chung-Hee stared at them.

"God damn that was a close call," Scott yelled.

"You're not kidding," Chung-Hee said.

Dawn sat next to Jon-Jon who still hadn't woken up.

Judy looked back at her, "He's going to be okay, Dawn. Jon's a tough guy and he'll pull through. He must've hit his head pretty hard. Just give him time, and keep his head up."

"Thanks, Judy. He better pull through. I'm starting to like him."

"Don't start getting soft, now."

"I'm not. Women like me don't get soft."

"How's your nose?" Joseph yelled over to his brother.

"Hurt's like a bitch, man."

"You break it?"

"Yeah, I think so. Feels like it, for sure," he said, licking the blood from his upper lip.

"Could be worse."

Eddie didn't want to think about it. Damn right it could've been worse. Him, his brother, and his mother could all be dead by now. All the suffering, the heartache, and the surviving these last days would all be for naught. If that was the case he would've chosen to be eaten on day one and just get it over with, but luckily they were still alive. Hanging on to the roof racks of a stolen truck and being stalked by the living dead, but alive.

Was it worth it, he wondered, and thought it had to be. Surely this was better than the alternative. Surely this was better than being one of the living dead.

19 FREE LUNCH

Abdul sped through the path along the road, bobbing and weaving out of the way of bushes and low-hanging branches. He continued to look for an opening that would allow them to get back onto the road but none presented themselves so he stayed the course. The kids thought the ride was fun and squealed in delight when Abdul hit a large bump, sending them up in the air.

"He's still not awake." Dawn said somberly, stroking his hand.

"He'll be fine," Judy reassured. "Janice, how's your head? Are you feeling okay?"

"Oh, I'm okay. Just a bit of a bump. The older I get the easier it is to bleed. Believe it or not I've bled worse from paper cuts."

"You're a tough woman. When we stop—if we stop, I'll see if I can scrounge up some Ibuprofen, or maybe something stronger if either of you need it. You might start feeling sore later, once the adrenaline wears off."

"My neck is already starting to hurt," Dawn said.

"At my age, I don't know what's a new pain or an old pain," she smiled, without even realizing it.

"How about you, Chung?"

"I'm good. A little cramped over here, but I can't complain."

"Good."

Scott rolled down the window and shouted to Eddie and Joseph on the roof, "How you guys holding up?"

"Just great!" Eddie yelled back.

"I keep getting hit by these fucking branches!"

"Sorry—doing the best I can!"

After an hour or so of slow moving on the side of the road the incline softened and the congestion of abandoned vehicles lessened allowing the two-car convoy to get back on the road.

Abdul pulled over to the side and slowed down. Scott pulled up next to him and rolled down the window.

"Scott, do you think it would be better to look for a new vehicle now, or continue moving forward?"

"I don't know. What do you guys think, up there?"

Eddie slid over to the edge, "I can hang on as long as we have to. Joe's fine too. I'd rather keep going and get some more distance between us and the deaders we left behind."

"Might as well keep going," Frankie joined in, "at least while the road is clear. Ya know? Go as far as we can. Then when it gets congested again, we'll have a better chance of finding another truck. More to choose from and shit."

"Makes sense," Scott agreed. "Chuck, whaddya think? Can you hold on longer?"

"Yeah, just don't go too fast guys, and no sudden breaking, please—we could go flying."

"Good point."

"After you, Abdul," Scott said.

"Okay, guys, hold on."

Eddie stared off to the side at the ever moving and changing landscape. Sparse trees littered the hills, industrial buildings bled into the grey of the sky and it all coalesced into a blurry image raking across his eyes.

Now more than ever the world seemed to be dying. Autumn always brought with it a sense of change, but now, coupled with the insanity that was the living dead that change seemed more permanent. Each falling leaf was a breath from a dying world, each tree a decaying limb. The roadways were clogged arteries that pulverized a still-beating heart, unaware of the massive attack that would soon sweep its tissue and leave it cold.

Maybe the clouds themselves would stay gray and fall out of the sky, blanketing the earth in a morbid dust-like haze.

"This sucks!" Joseph yelled, spitting bugs out of his mouth.

"It's a free lunch!"

Joseph held on to the roof racks with one hand, squeezing tighter than ever, as he used his other hand to wipe away the bugs that were smattering his face and collecting in his growing, but spotty, beard.

The idea of having to eat bugs to survive was not a new one. It was something he thought about quite a number of years ago while watching a television show that paid good money for people to eat insects. The show was supposed to be about facing fear, but in reality it was just about grossing out the audience so that they would be too disgusted to change the channel.

There were many similar shows Joseph watched when he could fit in time for television. Shows like Survivorman, Fear Factor, Man VS The Wild, and plenty more, and when Joseph came across an episode dealing with the ever-popular bug eating his stomach would turn and his mind would produce a scenario in which he had to eat bugs to survive.

In these machinations of his mind he would get as far as putting the bug in his mouth and upon feeling its legs touch his tongue he would throw up. Just thinking about it make him sick, and now, picking bugs out of his mouth he wondered how much longer it would be before that little nightmare became a reality. He still didn't know if he had what it took to eat a bug to live.

He could wipe his ass with leaves. He could forego bathing and neglect his hygiene. He could ration food, drink tepid tap water, and sleep in cars. He could kill the hell out of deaders, and he was able to keep his sanity mostly intact as he dealt with the grief over the fallen members of his family.

He turned his head to the side and tried not to think about it.

20 BIG BAD WOLF

Sarah and Jim sat near the window most of the day. Jim was nervous with how many deaders had been visible today. This was more than he'd seen in a number of days and he attributed it to he and Sarah attempting to flee earlier. They lingered far longer than they had been and a number of them had even come to the home clawing at it and shambling around, searching for a way in.

It kept both of them in a state of unease. Jim's mind was taken off his earlier dark thoughts and now focused on the deaders outside. They needed something big to divert their attention. He hoped a car would drive by, a gunshot would go off—hell, he didn't care what it was, so long as it made them go away.

Sarah grabbed the binoculars from Jim's desk and peered outside once again. She paused on each of the deaders. Taking in their grotesque appearances and their individual nuances distorted through the lens of death; one deader walked with his arm bent in front of him as if shielding his eyes with his forearm; another dragged its leg along the pavement and shrugged it's shoulder; one had facial tics; another was buck-naked and pale, her milky white skin contrasting against the dried blood that covered her forearms and hands that evidently poured from the gashes in her wrists.

She saw another one in the distance. There was something familiar about the deader and as it stepped out of the shadows his face could be seen more clearly.

"No…"

His eyes were wide. His cheeks sunken in and the skin of his lips shriveled tightly around his teeth.

"Oh God, no…"

"What? What's wrong?"

His shirt was in shreds and covered in dried blood. She could see his innards hanging out from underneath it and draping over his pants down into the street.

"Oh, fuck."

"Let me see."

His intestinal track dragged dryly along the black top, shredding more with each step.

"Goddamnit."

"Here, give me the binoculars."

It was Boone.

"I don't see anything special. What was it? What did you see?"

She was crying now, "Boone, my friend."

"Shit. He's out there?" He felt stupid even as the question came out of his mouth but there it was.

She nodded, putting her hand over her lips.

"I-I'm sorry. Jeez, that's awful," Jim didn't know what else to say. He was grasping for something. Anything. "Why don't you go lay down? I'll keep an eye on things. You should rest up."

"Yeah, okay," she said, as she walked out of the room looking just as pale and hollow as the dead things in the street.

The daylight seemingly took forever to die, but in the dusk the only thing that changed was how much of the dead Jim could see. He knew they were out there. Scraping at the door, prodding at the siding, walking down the streets. They knew he was in there. Somehow, they knew it and it creeped Jim the fuck out. He sat at the top of his stairway, listening to the sounds of the dead as they inspected the home. He could hear Sarah sleeping now, too. She went from sobbing to snoring, snoring to sobbing, and then back again to sobbing.

He looked back to the window, too afraid to go over and look out. It was a window into hell—the window of his tomb.

This must be hell, Jim thought.

Would it get any better?

Would it get any worse?

***

Sarah slept till daybreak and she woke with a feeling that could only be described as numb. The tears of yesterday were gone and it would seem the well had run dry. She wasn't all that sad anymore—just numb—hollow.

There was a burning feeling in her stomach. Hunger. But she didn't feel like doing anything about it. She was numb and hungry and at least being hungry meant she still felt something. Despite everything it meant she was still alive, and she guessed that was something.

She walked out of the room and jumped back when she found Jim asleep on the floor at the top of the staircase. He was curled up into a fetal position and looked so peaceful in that way that only sleep could offer.

She sat down next to him, and hearing the creak of the floor he woke up with a start.

"Morning," she offered.

"Hey," he said, groggily, wiping the drool from the corners of his mouth.

"Fell asleep on the stairs, I see."

"Yeah, I guessed I just passed out."

Then they heard the rumbling of a truck down the street, and they both smiled at each other.

"Come on!"

They ran to the window to see if they could catch a glimpse but they saw nothing and the noise faded away.

"Fuck."

"At least it might draw their attention away from us."

"Yeah, I guess."

"That's a good thing. It'll give us some breathing room."

Then the doorbell rang.

21 NOTHING BUT DARKNESS

From Eddie's vantage point he could see a clearing form in the landscape. There were tall apartment complexes in the distance framed out by a warehousing district. Further up, and closer to the road, as it turned into an overpass crossing a bisecting highway was a large cemetery with what looked like deaders walking around its grounds. Eddie pounded on the roof a few times and Scott slowed the truck down. He honked the horn to alert Abdul and in a moment both vehicles came to a stop in the road that overlooked the cemetery.

"What is it?" Scott called out.

"Look over there."

Eddie pointed out the cemetery and watched intently as deaders pulled themselves out of the earth. He couldn't believe what he was seeing. Joseph was watching as well, as was everyone else in the group by now save Carrie and the children.

These were nothing like the dead they've seen so far. Some of these things rising up from the earth were dead for a long time— some for decades, some longer, and of course some for less.

Somehow, Eddie thought, this was worse than the recently deceased coming back to life. Way worse.

The first days the news outlets had been reporting incidents of reanimation as rare viral outbreaks. Some had simply called it The Sickness. Others swore it was a large-scale terror attack using bio-weapons and chemical agents. In the end it was all noise. Nobody had known anything about what was happening. The dead digging themselves out of their graves however, cemented in Eddie's mind that it couldn't be a virus. This was no sickness. This was no bio-weapon. This was just straight up fucked.

"Damn bro," Joseph said, "now that's fucked up."

Scott climbed up the truck to get a better look and regretted doing so. "All that hard work embalming them, and for what?"

"Man, you can make a joke in any situation, huh?"

"If you can't laugh now, when can you?"

Eddie shook his head.

"Think about how many chemicals went into those bodies to keep them from rotting. Shit… all us embalmers did was end up making them in better shape to come back and get us. If we didn't replace their blood with embalming fluids most of them would be nothing but dirt and bones. Don't you see the irony? Our rituals for self-preservation—even if only of our appearance after death—may be what ensures our destruction."

"And you can laugh at that?"

"Yup."

They watched for a bit longer, in rapt attention, as the long dead awoke from their supposed eternal rest. Then, realizing a few abandoned cars were nearby, they searched for one they could drive away in.

Frankie sat on the roof of the SUV staring out at the dead, seemingly unblinking. He wished he had a cigarette, not that he smoked, or a drink—anything that would give his hands something to do before they found a gun and shoved it into his mouth.

Jon-Jon is running. There is nothing but darkness behind him. He can hear screams of agony all around. There is a woman laughing and an old man riding a bicycle naked in the street. People are taunting him and pointing at him with fingers like needles. The sky is full of eyes and the rain gutters are spilling over from tears. Dead swollen rats with long hairless tails flow along curbs to clog the storm drains.

Now he is in the ocean. The water is freezing. His father is telling him to swim. Screaming at him. "If you don't swim, you'll drown! You don't want to drown do you?"

He can't answer. His mouth is full of water. He is going under. This is it. His mother is down there, shimmering like the scales of fish, moving as if one with the water.

She looks beautiful.

There is a hand at his throat and a tentacle at his foot. The eyes in the sky are staring at him. They are angry. Their tears are salty. Below him is inky blackness. The tentacles are pulling him down into the obsidian nightmare.

His mother smiles. She is proud of her little boy. Drowning. He kicks his feet and pushes his hands against the water.

His lungs hurt. They need air. He is going to die down there in the cold waters.

Then there is air. His mother is gone, his father is clapping, and little Jon-Jon is treading water.

Jon and his father are at a bar. He has cancer. It doesn't look good. He has only ever seen his father cry for once before. He's crying now, not because he's dying but because he believes he will see his wife again soon. "Very soon," he tells his son, and this makes him happy.

Jon is alone. He is drinking. He is drinking alone and always drinking. He is always alone. He is sitting on a barstool with three fingers of whiskey in a glass.

He's a regular here. This is oblivion.

The darkness comes again. It is all around him. Icy water is flooding the floor. He orders another drink. Two fingers. A tentacle comes out of the darkness for each one, wrapping itself around him.

"Last call."

He orders just a finger, but the bartender left him the bottle hours ago. It sits empty in front of him.

He forgets he's alone.

He forgets how dark it is.

The tentacles pull him into the darkness.

It smells like wet earth and mold.

Jon-Jon is running again. He is ten years old and doesn't understand why his mother is dying. Jon-Jon is running. There is nothing but darkness ahead of him.

22 SOMETHING WICKED

Sarah and Jim stared at each other in disbelief.

"One of them must've hit the doorbell."

"Yeah, that's just weird though. I haven't heard the doorbell ring for—well, since the first few days of all--"

The doorbell rang again and then was followed by a thunderous banging. A deliberate three bangs that only another living person would do.

They returned to staring at each other.

"Maybe someone from your group saw us come here?"

"I dunno…maybe?"

"Let's go check it out."

They slowly descended the stairs, Jim taking the lead and Sarah nervously following behind.

Jim peered through the peephole and a dead man was smiling at him. Jim jumped back in shock. Sarah stepped forward and took a look as well. The dead man was now cocking his head to the side but continuing to grin his yellow-toothed grin.

Sarah started shaking and backing away to the steps.

"No…no, what the fuck? How? What? What's happening?"

"Please don't tell me that's your friend?"

"No. T-that's the guy who killed my friends."

The door rattled in its jamb as the dead man on the other side pounded it with his fist, "Let me in, let me in, little pig!"

"This can't be happening!"

"He can't get in, okay, it's locked. He's…wait a minute…since when do zombies talk? That dude looks dead as shit. And the other zombies aren't trying to eat him."

"This can't be real."

"Hey, piggy, let me in now and I'll make it quick."

"FUCK YOU!"

"Such a flirt, girlie. Don't worry I'll be seeing you in a bit and then we can finish what we started."

"Go to hell!"

"This is hell. How 'bout you Jimbo? I'll let you run free if you let me in right now."

Jim hesitated and Sarah could see him thinking it over. She began to back up the stairs shaking her head and whimpering.

"Get lost dirt bag."

"Your loss, kid."

Jim turned to Sarah, "How did that thing know my name?"

"What?" She asked, not realizing that he'd called Jim out by name.

"My name, he knew my fucking name! What is he?"

"I don't know! He's one of them, but he's different. He's still himself, he can talk…"

The sound of the truck starting ended both of their trains of thought.

"Is there another way out of here?"

"There's a back door but I boarded it up cause it's mostly glass."

"A way out the windows? Maybe we can jump to something?"

The truck roared as it sped toward the house. A crashing noise and the sound of crushing aluminum filled the house. He was driving through the garage door!

"Let's try for the kitchen downstairs, maybe we can get out the window."

They ran as the sounds grew more chaotic. The noise of the truck filled the house.

There was a small window behind the sink in the kitchen overlooking the backyard. Jim ran to it and opened it up. He knocked the screen out but while doing so he noticed that if he climbed out the window he'd land right into the arms of the living dead.

"Fuck. It's no good. Back upstairs!"

The noise of the truck seemed to settle and the sound of feet over the garage door took its place.

"There in!"

They were in mid-stride as the door to the garage burst opened. It had been locked, but Ben, the dead man with the yellow smile, kicked it open in one shot. His strength appeared to have grown but he knew it was only because he didn't feel the pain of his movements. Had he been alive he'd have felt his ankle sprain, and his muscles pull and tear. He'd have felt the shattering of his heel and he would recoil in pain instead of following through and making his grand entrance.

"Jimbo, nice to meet ya."

They stopped dead in their tracks and backed into the kitchen. Jim opened the draw of silverware and grabbed the largest knife he could. Sarah grabbed a dirty pan from the sink.

"Stay back you sicko!"

"Hey, you know what, I'm a good sport. Go ahead…run."

"What? You're just going to let us run out of here?"

"Out of the house? No. But go ahead, run upstairs. I'm guessing that's where the bedroom is, right?"

Sarah's face went rigid with disgust.

"Not like you got any real options. I'll even back up a step. There. Now go ahead and run."

"Fuck it." Jim took off in a sprint and Ben began to clap his hands and laugh. His laugh sounded like a smoker coughing up a lung.

Sarah, not seeing any other choice ran right behind Jim, and swatted at Ben as she ran past. The pan hit him in the elbow and he made no gesture to show it even touched him.

"Okay, now let's have some fun," Ben called out as he ran up the stairs behind them.

Sarah shrieked in terror as she felt his footfalls behind her.

23 BACK ON COURSE

Chuck was following behind the three-vehicle convoy in an old Toyota Corolla. The four men felt like clowns in a clown car but even that was better than holding onto the roof racks of a SUV speeding down the debris covered roadways.

The roads were far worse than any apocalyptic movie any of them had ever seen. Even The Road Warrior paled in comparison to the landscape of disaster that lay before them.

Heading north, much like heading to Titan City, seemed like another pipe dream. They hadn't been on the road a day and already their collective hope was diminishing. Totaling the van and nearly killing Jon-Jon left them road weary and worse for the wear.

Eddie felt as if he aged ten years as he checked his face in the cosmetic mirror in the cars sun visor. The dark rings and hard lines obscured the youthful man who only weeks ago still thought of himself as nothing more than a kid in a man's body.

"You going to put on some eyeliner?"

"You got some?"

Chuck shifted uncomfortably, but then Eddie and Joseph laughed.

"You think the congestion will get any better once we're out of Jersey?"

"I don't know, I figure it would, right? We do have one of the most densely populated states. I'm thinking maybe Massachusetts will be about the same, but I haven't thought much more about anything other than getting out of Jersey. I guess it all depends on what roads we can travel on and how far they are away from the bigger cities."

Chuck nodded, "One thing at a time then I guess."

The convoy moved swiftly through the congested roadway. The road seemed to have a rhythm all it's own. Areas where the road was clear, then congested, then a few sparse autos, then burned out husks and wrecks, and emptiness. It was cyclical. Driving through it you could almost picture how some of it played out. Drivers trying to run each other off the road, others bumping slower drivers to speed it up or get out of the way. Too many egos, too many emotions, and not nearly enough lanes.

On the empty bits of the road one could notice the trees. Tall and hopeful. Leaves falling to the ground with the most vibrant colors ever seen. Even the blue of the sky seemed particularly bright. The clouds were sparse and blended too well with smoke and ash from the fires of a hell on earth.

Frankie slept a dreamless sleep. His head rocked with the motion of the vehicle. His eyes opened on occasion and when he figured out he was still stuck in a nightmare he closed his eyes again, hoping harder with each time that he would dream of a better place, or at least a better time.

Jon-Jon is running again. Darkness is all around. He is alone now. Everyone he loves is dead, and in turn everyone who loved him is dead. There is no greater loneliness. The tentacles lose all their might, the darkness loses its depth, and the cold loses its bite. Lightning strikes in his mind, but it's not lightning. His eyes are opening and his head aches. The memories, daydreams, and nightmares coalesce. Melding into one reality.

Jon is awake. His vision blurred, but only for a few waking moments. He hears his name. There is surprise and warmth accompanying it. His vision sharpens and he knows where he is and who is around him.

"My head is killing me."

Dawn wraps her arms around him and hugs him so tight it's almost violent.

"Ow," he yelps.

"Sorry, just glad you're awake."

"You had us worried," Judy said.

"Not me. I knew you'd get up eventually. I just figured you'd try to eat us."

"Scott!" Judy slapped his arm.

"Is everyone okay?" Jon asked, remembering what had happened.

"Janice is a little banged up but other than that we're pretty okay."

"Sorry, Janice. That wasn't my intention."

"It's okay Jonathan. You took most of the damage, I think."

"Sure feels like it. We…we didn't lose anyone?"

"No."

"Thank Christ. How long've I been out?"

"Just a few hours."

"Are we back on course? Did I miss anything else?"

Scott answered, "Back on course and moving quick. We had to get out of there in a hurry after you flipped so a bunch of the guys had to hold on to the roof till we could get clear. They got a car now though, so were moving along."

24 DESPAIR

Jim turned the corner into his bedroom and bolted to the window. He tore off the blinds and opened it with a slam. He kicked out the screen. Sarah was right behind him.

"Go! Jump, he's right behind us!"

Jim hesitated. It was a long fall, and the dead were all over the place.

"Go!" She screamed.

"Ben stood in the doorway. His chest not heaving up and down like Jim and Sarah's. Running didn't make him out of breath—he had no need for breathing since his body had no longer any need for oxygen.

"Jimbo, don't you want to stay and join the party? I know you had some nasty ideas in your own head didn't ya?"

"No. No I didn't."

"You're a terrible liar, kid. She's a pretty girl, certainly you thought of tying her down and playing stuff the turkey. Actually, I know you did. You watched her while she slept. You wanted her. You didn't want to risk rejection or time by getting to know her. You just wanted to satiate your need."

"No...fuck you, I didn't."

"Fuck you. You did. I can see inside your head. You're just like me."

Sarah felt so small. She stood in the middle of two men that only wanted to use her for their own sick enjoyment. She had never wanted to die before. Now she prayed for it. She wanted so badly to be gone from this world. There was no deeper depth of despair in her mind.

"If you stick around, I'll let you have sloppy seconds. How's that sound? Better than jumping out a window, ain't it?"

Jim thought about it. It was better. If he jumped he'd probably end up getting eaten down there. If he stayed, maybe he could befriend this abomination. Maybe he could make it out of this alive.

Sarah saw the look in his eyes. She knew what he was thinking. She could see it in his body language as he shifted his weight back into the room. Before Jim shifted his weight entirely off the windowsill Sarah charged him and smashed him in the side of the head with the frying pan. His head smacked against the top sash and cracked the window. She hit him again and then kicked him out the window. He screamed as he fell.

Sara was putting her foot out the window, ready to jump down after him, but Ben came up from behind her and pulled her back by her hair.

"Not this time, bitch."

She screamed, making a hoarse noise that sounded more like an animals dying howl than anything remotely human.

He pulled her head back and smashed it into the window. Shattering the rest of the glass and cutting her face up in the same movement. Behind them the room filled with the dead that came into the home through the garage. They stayed back as if they were there only to bare witness.

"Let's watch," Ben said as he leaned out the window with Sarah, whom was now barely conscious.

The dead outside had gotten Jim when he fell to the ground. He landed on his leg, his femur rupturing the skin upon impact. His screams were drowned out as the dead things tore out his throat and his mouth filled with his own blood.

Ben watched eagerly as the dead things moved effectively over the body. Their bony fingers digging through the skin to get to the choice cuts. In minutes they had opened his stomach cavity and pulled out an endless buffet of intestines. The blood was so bright and his fatty tissue was a nasty yellow color that adorned many of the fingers of the dead as they pulled through it to get to his organs.

Several of the deaders worked on Jim's head and face, pulling out his eyeballs and tongue. One ate his nose as another chewed off bits of his cheek. Some of them bit at his head as two others pulled small clumps of brain from his ocular cavities.

By the time Jim's blood ran cold he had become one of the dead things. He was a ravaged mess of remains with no eyes. His guts poured out further once he sat up. The dead things moved away from him sensing he was now one of them. The lower part of his ribcage was visible and chunks of brain dropped out of his eye sockets. He shambled closer to what was his home and began to follow the dead as they sought a way in.

"Isn't that beautiful?"

Sarah wept. She knew she was as good as dead. She willed herself to die right there. She tried to shut her mind off. No matter how hard she prayed. How much she cried. How desperately she wanted to die. How badly she wanted to lose her mind and not be aware of what was happening was of no consequence. She was there. Her sanity intact and the fear of the horrors that this sick bastard had in mind for her was burning like a torch in a catacomb.

25 ARE WE THERE YET?

Yussef began to whimper that he was hungry. Alexis urged him to hold on as long as he could.

"We need to get somewhere safer," she insisted.

"There are some snacks in the back I believe," Abdul said.

The other children then realized that they too were hungry, and in moments the SUV was full of crying hungry children.

"Stop crying!" Carrie yelled.

"Don't yell at them like that," Alexis scowled at her.

"Then keep those fucking brats quiet! It's hard enough living like this without having to deal with them."

"You're way out of line, bitch, and if you keep it up you won't have to worry about the friggin' zombies because I'll tear your throat out by myself."

Chris started to cry again, and then so did Leela. The yelling scared them and confused them.

Carrie turned to her, "I'd like to see you try you skinny little--"

Abdul backhanded Carrie across the face, "That is enough. Shut up or get out. When we stop you can see about riding with the others."

"Bastard," she hissed, pressing a hand to her face, "how dare you."

"Stop it!" Stacey yelled, almost at tears herself. She sounded as if she'd yelled at a man hitting a woman before.

He glared at her, "Shall I pull over?"

She said nothing more.

Alexis had never seen a woman get smacked by a man like that, at least not in real life, and it shocked her. Carrie deserved it, and if Abdul hadn't done it Alexis was prepared to do worse. It must've shocked the children too; because they had quieted down a bit since it happened.

Stacey sat quietly, looking at Abdul in a different light. Her father and mother fought all the time. Her father had hit her mother a few times, her as well, but only when they fought. Most of the time they were happy. She missed her mother and father, even if her father was mean sometimes.

Alexis shifted the children aside and rummaged through the supplies in the back till she found some snacks for the kids to munch on. What she found was far from a meal, but it was enough to turn their crying into munching.

"Chew slowly and take your time eating, okay?"

They nodded in unison, but seemed to inhale the food.

"Think we'll be stopping soon?"

"I doubt it. We've been moving too well to stop. I know it's uncomfortable for all of us now, but the longer we can do this for, hopefully the better we'll be in the long run."

"Agreed, but try telling them that," Alexis said.

"Just stay strong, we're closing in on the state lines and night is drawing closer. They'll want to stop and set up camp. I think we'd all agree it's a bit too dangerous driving these roads at night with all the debris on it."

"Too bad this truck doesn't have a DVD player so I can keep them distracted. I think that would help a ton."

"I bet it would. When we set up camp later maybe we can give them something to do. Collect sticks or something. A task could prove distracting."

"That sounds like a blast."

"It would get them moving, and give them something to do."

"I know, just saying is all."

***

"Jon, now that you're up, let's talk about how we're going to cross the state line."

"Well, Scott," he scratched his head, "I didn't think that far ahead, at least not with any specifics other than north."

"You've got to be shitting me. That was the entirety of your plan? We went a long with this out of the hope you knew where you were going, that there was an idea, a destination, a fucking clue."

"Easy man, I had some vague ideas, but to tell you the truth, I didn't see any easy way. Or a clear way to get across considering how shitty the roads have been. I was thinking maybe we could take 287 into New York, or Connecticut, or maybe find a boat and cross the Hudson, you know, fucking whatever presented itself."

"Than you should've said that. You got me worked up now. So you want to head into New York, or shoot for Connecticut? 287 can take us to either or, actually we have to go through New York either way, but who knows what the hell that mess will look like."

"Don't care. Eddie suggested northeast, trying to stick to the coast. I like the sound of it, but can we even do it?"

"That would mean going into Connecticut, which gives us fewer options. The most direct way I think is 287 and onto the Tappan Zee bridge, unless we can find a ferry or boat to cross the Hudson. I'd rather keep our vehicles, though, but taking the bridge just sounds like a nightmare. I doubt we'd even be able to get to it."

"Let's give it a shot at least. Even if we can't do it we can still follow the Hudson up and go up and around. Head over to Palisades Park and take 87 into Albany."

"Maybe we can camp out in the park for a day and rest up," Judy suggested.

"I'm down for that. Might be a good place to scavenge for supplies. They have a boat dock there too, I think. It's starting to sound better than the bridge now."

"Yeah, but we should stay focused. We have a destination in mind, anything else is a distraction. The sooner we can get someplace safe, the sooner we can scavenge and stock up and fortify wherever we end up."

"Then keep driving. Let's see what the Tappan Zee has in store for us."

"I hate bridges," Judy said.

Dawn nodded in agreement, "yeah, me too."

Janice thought about the bridge. She'd only been over it a handful of times and remembered how anxious she would get being on it. The lanes were narrow and everyone seemed to speed over it. She wondered if they would chance walking over it if they couldn't get by in the vehicles. The bridge could be a good place to die.

She pictured herself walking over it, falling further behind from the others—she was older after all, who would think anything of it. The lanes were narrow and sure to be full of cars and trucks, maybe even debris. They would get close to the peak of the bridge. The group would splinter off. There would be too many distractions and everyone be looking forward rather than behind. Then maybe a deader would lurch out of a truck, or crawl from underneath one and grab her. She would scream, but she wouldn't do anything to stop it, she wouldn't even move. Just close her eyes and let the fucker have at her. Goodbye cruel world, hello paradise.

26 HEART OF THE MATTER

Sarah fought Ben with all she had, but what she had left wasn't much. Ben didn't so much as flinch with any of the blows Sarah was landing on his face. Her knuckles reddened, her wrist ached, and her strength waned. Ben laughed it off and threw her onto the bed with such force she smacked into the headboard.

The dead things stood in the room almost motionlessly, swaying in place gently.

Ben lunged on top of her and she screamed louder than she ever thought possible. It was useless, futile, and Ben knew it. He smiled a sickly grin. His lips were all ready chapping and shriveling. He was starting to look dead, which made any expression on his face infinitely more disturbing and unnatural.

"Come here sweetheart."

"Fuck you!"

"How's this sound. If you go along with this and act like you want it I'll be kind and kill you quickly. If you want to fight me and buck me the whole time, I'm gonna take my time. I'll kill you so slowly that you'll wish you were never fuckin' born."

"I won't give in to you."

"That's your choice, but know this: it doesn't fuckin' matter. I offered you mercy but if you want to suffer, then suffer you will."

He grabbed her by the hair. And began to lick at her neck. His tongue was dry and felt like sandpaper. His breath smelled like rot and when he went in to kiss her she bit his lip and tore a chunk of it off.

Ben didn't scream in pain. He only smiled. "I knew I liked you for a reason, girly."

She chewed the lip; hoping whatever kept him alive would kill her before he did.

The realization hit him almost immediately.

"You cunt! Give me that back!"

He grabbed her face, prying open her mouth, but the bitch already swallowed the two-inch flap of his lip.

"Fuckin' a girly. Guess you found a way of dying quicker, eh?"

Ben felt deflated, and Sarah almost triumphant.

"Still don't mean shit. I'm gonna make it hurt till yer one of us."

Then he punched her in the face, drawing blood and sending a jolt of pain across her teeth. He pulled out a knife and flipped it open. It was no bigger than the size of his palm, but it looked sharp, and when he held it up to his face and smiled it might as well have been a chainsaw.

He grabbed her by the throat and savagely cut her clothes off. Scraping, gouging, and slicing her with the knife as he did so. The more she fought the harder he hit her back. She was losing steam. The energy to fight back was depleting. Was it the dead flesh in her guts working it's magic? She didn't know, she didn't really care. She just wanted it over, and maybe if he hit her enough times she'd black out. So, she kicked him and hit him again. Enraging him. He gave her what she wanted and punched her again. This time breaking her nose and making her two front teeth loose and numb.

She wanted to feel numb all over. She found the strength to fight more. Ben knocked her two front teeth down her throat and made her whole mouth numb. She gagged and screamed but she still didn't pass out from the pain.

Ben began to pull his pants down. He willed himself to get hard, but failed miserably. He tried to push it in soft, but with the bitch squirming the way she was it would be impossible. He punched her several times. The face, the body, her thighs and her groin. His blows felt hard every time. Never softer, always the same intensity. He fought the urge to stab her and be done with it. He wanted to stretch it out. To really make it agonizing. Then he thought of something else he could do with the knife. He held it alongside his dead dick and began to ease it into her.

Her screams were unlike any he'd heard before. The pain took her breath away. Each thrust was a new hell and a new level of pain she'd never thought possible. It didn't take long before she finally passed out from it, but when she awoke the pain began again.

The dead filled the room. Mumbling nothings, wanting to groan and grunt, to pull and prod at the wound that was Sarah's womanhood. They wanted to rend her flesh and eat her innards. Pluck out her eyes and tear her throat out, but some force kept them at bay.

Ben ran the knife all along her body, wiping the vaginal blood all over her face. She whimpered, defeated, and dying slowly like a tiny white mouse in a snake's cage.

The knife went in deep. Agony atop agony. The dead thing that was Ben only seemed to smile wider. He could feel her slipping away from him, though. Whatever dark shit was in his blood was in hers and it was starting to take shape. He could see it like an aura, smell it, and taste it in her blood.

She would be one of the dead, not like him though, like the others.

She felt it too. A burning inside that was different from the physical hell she'd been in. It felt like every nerve ending was on fire. Like her guts were turning inside out. She couldn't wait to be done with all of this. *There could be nothing worse, could there?*

Ben straddled her. Sitting on her stomach. He lifted the small knife high. Sarah looked at him, barely able to focus, and didn't seem to care anymore about the pain and the promise of more. It was almost done. All of it.

He brought the knife down into her chest—between her breasts. He began to cut the flesh out. Digging in deep with the knife, prying the muscle from the bone. Her screams were nothing more than a reaction, muddled, and distorted. Her lungs were filling with blood and he was stuffing the skin and sinew into her mouth. He violently began to stick her with the knife, making a hole in her chest. Her sternum was proving to be laborsome for the small knife but he almost had it. Then after several more relentless blows he pulled her heart out and shoved it into her mostly toothless mouth, but she was already too dead to notice.

Moments later her eyes opened, but Sarah was gone and whatever remained, started eating her heart.

27 JUST THE WIND

Full dark was quickly falling on New Haven and Walter, Jeff and Barbara were heading back home with a bed full of looted supplies. Walter was surprised by how much they were able to pull together. He also knew, and his children agreed, that there was a lot more that they could gather up if they picked up tomorrow where they left off today.

Jeff wanted to see how the day went, though. He didn't want to be away for a full day again, but after they inventoried what they had found and calculated how long it would last he might think differently. He just hoped things had gone smoothly at home. They hadn't seen many deaders in the neighborhood, but there were a few. They avoided confronting them when possible, but that had rarely worked. They always seemed to home in on them.

"Shit, I just remembered. We were going to burn the bodies tomorrow."

"That we were. Shouldn't take us all day though. Hopefully a few hours—gonna stink to high heavens."

"I didn't even think about the stink. I'm going to want to shower."

"We might as well. Get everyone to shower up tomorrow. Then we can refill all the water supplies. Then rest up a bit I guess. My back will be useless come midday."

"You still want to do the fence?" Barbara asked.

"Yeah, that I do, maybe we can do a small run day after tomorrow. Hit a few houses on the way to Gupp's see if there's anything left we can get from there. I doubt too many people were picking up fencing posts and all that, if they even carried it."

"We can always rip off someone else's fence too."

"Yeah, but that would be a lot more work. Let's just hope they stocked something we can use."

They pulled up to the house, making sure not to run over the bodies strewn about the grounds, and from the outside all was dark. From a distance you could barely see it, only as you got closer and the moonlight highlighted the shape of the home did you know it was a home and not some abandoned house on an unkempt bit of property. It was disturbing how uninviting a home was without a porchlight on outside and some semblance of activity on the inside.

Laura and Maria came to the door to peer out. A warm light behind them backlighting their thin figures. Tommy, Sandra and Wally stood behind them, but Maria shooed them back into the house as Laura descended the steps to greet them.

"Took you long enough."

"It was worth it," Walter said. "I take it all went well here?"

"It was pretty quiet. Pretty lonely too."

Walter kissed her on the forehead, "Good to know a little distance still makes the heart grow fonder."

"Some things never change. Can I help lug this stuff in?"

"Knock yourself out. Anything to eat?"

"I'll make whatever you and the kids want."

"Kids?" Barbara feigned indignation.

"Just like you'll always be," Laura smiled.

They all grabbed something from the bed of the truck and brought it inside. Taking several more trips before it was all unloaded. Everyone washed their hands while Laura put on a pot of boiling water. Jeff tossed his mother a box of spaghetti as the kids tugged on his shirt for him to come and play with them. They were building forts and playing puzzles.

Barbara dug out a jar of Ragu and put it on the counter, "I know you hate this stuff ma, but just use it—we don't have all day to make sauce."

"Ragu? It really is the end of the world."

"Mom's got jokes."

"I wasn't trying to be funny."

Walter dried his hands on a rag, "Did we snag any meatballs?"

"Mama Lucia. Over there."

Laura rolled her eyes and gave a big sigh.

"Oh, come on. Old Mama Lucia isn't that bad."

"With your tastes you'd think I never cooked for you people."

After what had turned out to be a rather satisfying dinner, Maria volunteered to help inventory the newly acquired supplies so that Jeff could play with the kids for a while. She, and Barbara started bringing it all downstairs while Walter drank down another glass of water. He was parched, sore, and more tired than he'd likely admit. Laura started to clean up the table and wash the dishes. Jeff handed his mother a plate and headed to the living room.

Jeff sat down amongst his children. The room was lit by a single lamp that made everything look warm and inviting while casting deep dark shadows in the recesses of the room. He sat down and crawled into a blanket that was tucked under a couch cushion and draped over an end table, effectively making a fort. It was far from the forts he and his sister used to make when they were younger, but Tommy was only just starting into the fort loving years. He was sure that he would guide his younger siblings into fort crafting for years to come and surpass what he did in his youth. Jeff chuckled at his train of thought, but found it comforting to know his mind could still find happy avenues to explore.

In the midst of playing the fort was torn down several times, and it was rebuilt several times as well. Sandra was getting tired, as could be exhibited when things didn't go her way and she would break down, having mini tantrums until Jeff could redirect her attention to something else. It would soon be time to put the kids to bed, and Jeff couldn't help but think of hitting the sheets early too, but he wanted to play with his kids a little longer. It had been a long day and the next few days would be equally as long.

Scrrrrtch. Scrrriiiittch.

Jeff's eyes widened and he looked about the room alertly.

"What's that daddy?" Sandra asked, her eyes wide.

"Probably just a tree hitting the house, kiddo, it's windy tonight."

"Is it zombies, dad?" Tommy asked, "Cause I'm not afraid of them. We can fight them together."

"Just the wind, okay. Keep playing. I'm going to see what mommy is doing because it's time for bed soon okay."

"I can be Mutant Man," Tommy said, "and you can be Cyborg-face!"

"That sounds like fun, but I'm pretty sure it's bed time."

"Oh, man. Do we have to go to sleep now?"

"Yes, you know you have to."

Scrrrtchhh. Skkkkkrrrrrr.

Jeff walked back into the kitchen. It was empty and everything was neat and clean. The basement door was open and Jeff went to the stairs.

"Dad. I think something's outside. Maria, can you bring the kids up and put them to bed?"

"Something, or a lot of something?"

"Just something, I think if there were a lot, we would've seen them coming when we were driving back."

"Probably," Walter agreed.

"I'll bring them up now," Maria said, walking passed and touching Jeff's arm, "be careful, okay?"

"Of course."

Walter turned to his wife and daughter, "Can you two finish this up okay by yourselves?"

"Don't be silly, Walter. But please be careful."

"I know, I know."

***

When Jeff left, Tommy stood up and pushed his chest out. "I'm not afraid of zombies."

"What's a sommy?" Sandra asked.

"Space monsters."

"Ohhhhh," Sandra nodded.

Tommy walked over to the boarded up window where the scratching sound came from. He put his ear on the board and listened intently. His tiny heartbeat raced as he waited for a sound.

Sandra stood behind him, hands on her hips and her head cocked to the side, "Well?"

"Shh. I can't hear with you talking."

"Hmmph."

Little Wally walked over wanting to be a part of the fun as well.

Tommy continued listening but was now more relaxed, as he didn't hear anything. Maybe his father was right and it was just the wind. He was about to pull away when he could hear something scratch at the board on the other side of the house—Walter and Jeff had boarded up the inside and outside of the first level—his heart seemed to jump into his throat and he bounced back.

"Sommy?" Sandra asked.

"I—I think so," Tommy stammered.

"What are you kids doing?" Maria asked.

"Nothing."

Maria looked at the window and then looked at the three of them. Tommy looked terrified, Sandra excited, and Wally was in his own world as he headed back to the fort.

"Well, come on, it's time for bed. Let's go."

"Five more minutes?"

28 LOW ON OPTIONS

Scott led the convoy toward the Hudson. They were only a few miles away, but Scott doubted that they would be able to get close to the bridge. He could only imagine what hell occurred on it in the first days. He'd seen news footage of roadway congestion on tunnels and bridges as early as what the media had deemed 'Day One' and knew that what they would find would be no better. Only by now most of the people and deaders would be gone, or at least they had hoped so. Maybe a few stragglers, but what reason would they have to haunt the bridge?

Congestion on the road began to build again. More remnants of accidents, more cars, more clutter, more things to get in the way, and more things to avoid.

"Not looking too good," Scott said.

"Think we should try getting onto 287 or 87?" Judy asked.

"Not sure. It's the most direct way, but I think the more travelled of roads."

"Doesn't look like we can make it much further."

"Let's pull over and see what the gang thinks."

"Scott, between us in here, what do you think we should?"

"What do you mean? About the Tappan Zee, or…?"

"Yeah, man, about the bridge about it all. I think you are probably the smartest out of us all--"

"I wouldn't say--"

"Of course you wouldn't, but I think you are. So I want to know, do you think we're going about this the right way?"

"Yes. I think we are. I think moving out of a heavily populated area makes sense. Moving as quickly as we can and putting distance between those places and us also makes sense. I think we would be just as safe heading into upstate New York as opposed to following the coast all the way up to Maine and beyond. I think we are putting ourselves in danger the closer we get to any major city, but that's all relative. The truth is we don't know enough to make a smart move. Smarts is only good when there's information. Till we have enough information the best thing to do is go with our guts and keep doing what we're doing."

"So you think we should try for the bridge, or head toward the Palisades?"

"Bridge. We're closer to the bridge. It makes sense to check it out. We don't have a lot of options so we should keep them open."

"See, I told you you were smart."

"I think you hit your head too hard."

Scott slowed down and came to a stop. The rest of the convoy followed suit. Scott, Judy, and Jon stepped out of the car. The others met them in the middle of the road.

"What's up?" Eddie asked.

"We're running out of road here. What do you think about giving 287 a go?"

"Do we have much of a choice?"

"Not if we want to get into Connecticut. Our best bet is to shoot for the Tappan Zee Bridge."

Frankie came out of his stupor after hearing that, "Wait a fucking minute, since when are we hopping onto a fucking bridge?"

"Since we decided to go north," Jon-Jon said.

"If I wanted to kill myself, I would just do it."

"Guys, it's really the best way to do this. Obviously if we get there and it's fucked we move on and try something else."

"What else?" Eddie asked.

"We either have to cross the Hudson or go around it. Going around it means going into upstate and moving northwest—the opposite direction of where we said we wanted to go. You said you wanted to stick to the coast and move up it quickly, well, this is it."

"Any other way to cross the Hudson?"

"Boat."

"That sounds like a better idea already. Does it not?"

"At first, sure," Scott conceded, "but consider this; all the things that make the bridge dangerous, are gone, or should be. No one should be left on the bridge. No people. No deaders. Now that doesn't mean we can just drive up it. I'm willing to bet once we get close enough we'll have to hoof it."

"This keeps getting better," Frankie looked around incredulously.

"Abdul, whattya you think. You haven't said shit."

"I'm not opposed to the bridge, but I think the boat sounds like a far better idea. If we are looking for the simplest solution to go north while avoiding the dead, than how is the bridge better? I don't see these things swimming after us."

"Do any of us know how to drive a boat?"

"I could manage." Chuck said, raising his hand.

"Okay, we have a captain. But now we have to find a boat big enough for all of us. Chuck, would you be able to pilot a boat of that size?"

"Might be a bit rougher of a ride, but yeah."

"Okay, and if we can't find a boat of that size does anyone else know how?"

"I could run the basics by whoever would want to give it a shot. It's really not that tough. I think we can definitely get across the Hudson. Taking it into the ocean and up the coast, that's a different story."

"I still think getting to the bridge would be safer than searching the nearby docks. We would be going into populated areas. Let's at least consider it till we can see what the bridge looks like. We have to go in that direction anyway."

"All right, Scott, take us to 287 and get us to the bridge. When we get there we need to know what the hell we're going to do, so everyone make up your minds by the time we get there and we'll take a vote." Eddie said. "Anyone have anything they want to bring up now?"

"Yes. Carrie, the woman riding with me no longer wishes to ride with me. Is there any room for her elsewhere?"

"Nope. Why?"

"She is a horrible woman. She was screaming at the children because they are hungry, Alexis was fighting with her as well, and I slapped her to shut her up."

"Tell her she better get along. We can't afford to fight amongst ourselves," Scott said, surprised that he'd hit her.

"Do you have food for the kids?" Eddie asked.

"They had some snack food, but they need a real meal. They are getting restless and if we are going to foot the bridge, they will need to eat before that. Just on the physicality of the task. I'm not even sure if they'll be able to do that anyway, especially the youngest, Chris."

"Shit, I didn't even think about that." Scott said.

"We can always carry them on our shoulders, right?" Jon asked.

"If you're volunteering your shoulders, sure."

"Well, it doesn't change anything now. We still have to get to the bridge. I think we can get there in under an hour, depending on what 287 looks like anyway."

29 NANCY NEDERMEYER

Jeff and Walter climbed the stairs, leaving Laura and Barbara to finish inventorying and putting away the new supplies.

"I really hope it's just one or two."

"You're starting to sound like a crybaby."

"Nah, just starting to sound like an old man."

"You've always sounded like an old man."

Walter gave him a light jab in the kidney, "Shut up and get suited up."

As Maria escorted the kids upstairs Walter and Jeff suited up to go outside. Walter slung the rifle over his shoulder, but hoped he wouldn't have to use it. The more he thought about it the more he thought the dead hunted by sound, and with the evening as quiet as it was, the crack of rifle fire might as well be a dinner bell.

Armed with a baseball bat and a shovel the father and son duo stepped cautiously outside. Jeff switched on his flashlight and held it out in front of him. Jeff led the way around to the side of the house and Walter followed a few paces behind him, clutching the shovel and ready to swing.

Scrrrrtch. Skkkkrrrrrrrrtttchhhh.

They could hear the scratching, but the couldn't see anything yet. They made to the next corner of the house. To where the window was in the living room. Jeff ran the flashlight over the body of dead woman as she turned to acknowledge them. Her hands and forearms were covered in dried blood. Her hair was caked to the side of her head and wore a grimace of torn flesh and cracked teeth. Her body was covered in dirt, blood and bruises. Her cellulite jiggled as she staggered toward them.

"Jesus…"

"I'll get her," Walter said.

Walter stepped up and away from the house, hoping to draw her to him. Jeff stepped back a bit and she started moving for Walter, her mouth opening like a torn scab. As she stepped closer it dawned on Walter that he knew this woman, or thought he did. She looked a lot like Norman Nedermeyer's oldest daughter, who had lived across town. The last time he'd seen her was over a year ago at Norman's wake. His thoughts caused him to hesitate a moment, allowing her to gain a step more than she would have if he had been staying focused. He stepped back, nearly stumbling, but was able to raise the shovel before she grabbed him and knocked her to the ground.

"You okay, dad?"

"Fine," he said, stepping on the woman's chest, "remember Nedermeyer who passed away not too long ago?"

"Yeah?"

Walter put the shovel against her throat as if he were about to break ground, "Well, this is his daughter." He put his weight down on the blade of the shovel and drove it though her throat. He had to do it a few more times before the head came completely off.

"Nancy?"

"That's her. Nancy Nedermeyer. They had a thing about naming everyone with an 'N'."

"Her brother was Nathan, and they had a dog named Nestle."

"Yeah, I remember Nathan from school—he used to catch a lot of shit for that. Kids made fun out of him all the time. Till he turned into a 6 foot hulk of course."

"Well, Nancy, say hello to your father," Walter said.

"I hate how they twitch," Jeff commented, pointing at her hands that looked as if they could be typing something on a keyboard."

"It is unsettling."

"Let's finish the walk, and then go back around."

"After you."

Jeff led the way again, flashlight in hand, and Walter just behind. As they walked past Nancy Nedermeyer her jaw slowly gnashed the air.

The children were in bed with Maria. They had all put on their pajamas, but there clothes were laid out on the floor in case they needed to get changed and leave the house in a hurry. They were under the covers with a candle on each nightstand, as Maria read them a few small books to help them fall asleep. They each got to pick one of their favorites, and Maria read Wally's first since he usually fell asleep quickly.

Laura and Barbara had just finished listing all of the new supplies and had put it all away orderly and kept the stuff that would go bad the soonest towards the front of the shelves. They had estimated that all the new food and beverages could buy them, if used somewhat sparingly, an additional two weeks on top of what they already had.

"Let's head upstairs sweetie," Laura said.

"I'm ready for bed."

"You should get some rest while you can."

"Easier said than done. Seems like the more I sleep the more times I wake up with nightmares."

"I would suggest you take something, but I guess nowadays that would be a bad idea. We need to be able to get out quickly if we need to, and I doubt your brother would want to carry you over his shoulder while you were snoring."

"I don't snore."

"Not lately, I guess."

30 END OF THE ROAD

As they drove along the New York State Thruway on 287 the road began to clog up. The southbound side was the equivalent of a parking lot. Scott slowed down and continued forward.

"It's already getting really congested," Scott said.

"Getting pretty creepy. The slower we drive through it the more I expect to see someone in one of the cars," Judy said.

"Do you know how much further it is?"

"It's not that much further. I think it's only a few more miles. We should be able to see it any minute."

"I doubt we--"

"Shit!"

"What? What is it?"

"End of the road. This is as far as we can drive."

"Fuck, man."

"What are we going to do Scott?"

"Turn around, or walk it."

"How far of a walk?"

"Might be only 10 or so miles to the bridge."

"So that would take us how long to walk?" Dawn said, trying to figure out the math in her head.

"If it were just us adults I'd say only a few hours. But there's no way the kids could keep up with us."

"What if we were to carry them, or have them sit on our shoulders?"

"At best we'd have to take turns, it would be quicker than having them walk it, but I remember taking my niece to the mall a few years ago when she was a toddler, I had her sit on my shoulders. We walked around like that for maybe 40 minutes. My neck was soar and my lower back was killing me."

"Well, we've got to do something. We also need to make up our minds."

"That's right. Eddie wanted us all to know if we would stick to the bridge or try for Palisades Park. This may be scary. It's dangerous as hell, but there's no promise that going for the Palisades will be any better. I say we try for the bridge."

"Yeah, fuck it, let's go for the bridge," Jon-Jon said.

"I'm in." Dawn said.

"I'm in too. Janice, we understand if you want to talk it over with your sons."

"Thanks Judy. I'll vote for the bridge as well, though. And if I know my sons they'll be thinking the same thing. My husband always used to say 'no guts, no glory'."

"Good motto, don't know if the old me would've agreed though."

Inside the next vehicle a very similar discussion was going on.

"We should just go for the boats. Get out on the water. We're not going to see any deaders yachting it up."

"I agree with flip-flops. The bridge is too fucking dangerous."

"Fuck that. It'll be more dangerous getting to a marina than getting to the bridge."

"Okay, assholes, listen. It looks like one way or the other, we're walking to the bridge. From there we can scope out the marinas or the docks, or whatever. We'll be able to see what we're getting into and we can course correct then. The decision might be made for us when we get there."

"What if we can't agree? Do you think we might split off?"

"I don't know Chuck. Let's go find out," Eddie said as he opened the car door.

"This should be fucking great."

Carrie folded her arms and shook her head, "No. No freakin' way am I walking to a goddamned bridge! Have you all lost your mind?"

"Look, everyone is getting out of their vehicles. We are all going, if you want to stay here by yourself that's your decision."

"What about the kids? You think they'll be able to keep up with you? You'll get them all killed."

"Now you care about what happens to them?"

"You take them out there like this and you might as well put a gun to their heads now!"

"That's enough. I'm taking them out now. You want to help keep them safe then step up and come out with us."

"You're insane. You're all nuts."

Abdul handed her the keys, "Good luck."

She then went on a tirade, screaming about how stupid they were and how dead they would be.

Abdul moved to the back of the truck. He rummaged through the supplies they had and started organizing a pack to take with him. Alexis lead the kids out of the truck and joined him, doing the same. The kids started running around and acting up. Carrie sat in the passenger seat staring out the window with a look of contempt smeared across her plump face. Her cheeks were red from yelling.

Eddie walked over to the kids, mussing up Yussef's hair as he used to do to his own little siblings. He knelt down among the kids. "Hey, listen up guys. We're going to be taking a long walk, okay? We need you all to listen and to be strong. Can you all be strong?"

They nodded grimly.

Stacey said, "We've been strong."

"I want chocolate milk," Chris, the youngest of them, said.

"Me too, kiddo. And hopefully when we are all done with this big adventure we can find some chocolate milk. Maybe even some cookies. How's that sound?"

"Mmmm."

"I want a cookie now," Leela smiled.

"I want cookie," Chris said, looking around for one.

Nick laughed at the small boy, "There aren't any cookies yet."

"As soon as we find some. I promise. Maybe we'll find some on our walk."

The kids were now excited about their walk. Though if experience had taught Eddie anything, that wouldn't last.

Janice had been watching her son talking to the children. It made her heart swell with pride to see the compassion he still had in him. On the surface she likened him to looking like a soldier—stone-faced and determined—but she knew that inside was still her warm-hearted son. Despite how much he had lost in terms of his own family, he was still willing to keep on going, and to help these kids find someplace to be safe.

Maybe I'm just being selfish. Maybe I should be trying to help these kids and this group instead of giving up and waiting for death.

Janice felt something stirring in her chest. She wanted to help these kids make it. If she had died instead of her youngest children, she'd have wanted someone to take care of them—someone to help them. There was that stirring again—the will to live—rising up in her chest.

"Thanks," Alexis said.

"I should be thanking you. You're the one keeping these kids alive right now."

She blushed. "Hey, you guys lost all your shit, right?"

"Pretty much."

"Me and Abdul have taken everything we can carry. There's still plenty of stuff in here. Grab what you want and I'll let everyone else know to check it out before we head out."

"How about we eat some of these canned goods before we start moving. We'll all need the energy."

"Yeah, the kids were getting hungry earlier. That'd be good. I'll let everyone know."

Eddie held a can of Chef Boyardee in his hand, "Fucking cold raviolis."

"We have Spam, a can of corn, canned soups, it'll be a feast."

Eddie looked up, and Abdul smiled back at him, "I didn't think you had a sense of humor."

"I was being serious." Abdul said, still smiling.

31 STARTING TO PILE UP

Jeff was already awake when Walter painfully moved down the stairs. He was dressed and ready to go. Maria and the children were still asleep. Laura was getting dressed and Barbara was on watch till everyone woke up.

"You're finally up before me."

"Yeah, well, it happens every once and a while."

"It's only because my back is killing me already."

"We got a long day pops."

"I know. I'll take an Advil. Give me a few minutes will ya?"

"Take your time. I'm going to head out and get started."

"Go ahead. Be sure to drag them well away from the house. That stink gets in here and we won't ever get it out. And...be careful. Don't get too close."

"Go take your Advil."

Walter walked to the kitchen, the inflammation in his back causing him to lean forward as opposed to his usual back-straight-chest-out posture.

Jeff paused on the porch before descending the stairs. He could see at least two deaders on the horizon; they were little more than stark black silhouettes against a colorful morning sky, whether or not they were headed for him and his family he couldn't tell. He surveyed the day's work and didn't see how it would only take a few hours. There were bodies everywhere. There had to be at least two-dozen of them.

He descended the stairs, shovel in hand, and began to walk around the house making sure there wouldn't be any surprises. As he rounded the house, which was surprise free, he walked over to the shed and undid the latch.

He put down his shovel and swung open the double doors. He wheeled out the wheelbarrow, put his shovel in it, and began to toss a few other items in it as well; gloves, crowbar, rope, gas can—which was so heavy it almost tipped the wheelbarrow—and a dirty old painter's tarp.

By the time Jeff brought the wheelbarrow around his father was tying a bandana around his face like an old-timey bank robber.

"Took you long enough."

"If you're going to hassle me I'll call up my union rep."

"You leave your mother out of this."

"Only for her sake."

"What are you doing with that painter's tarp?"

"Well I figured it might be easier to roll them onto it and drop 'em in the barrow that way."

"Good thinkin'."

They went to work immediately on the task at hand. Jeff kicked the nearest deader to make sure it was really dead and all it did was twitch.

"Why do you think they twitch like that?"

"I dunno…maybe they're trying to get back up."

Jeff put down the tarp right next to the dead thing. Walter grabbed its legs and Jeff hesitantly grabbed it from its shoulders, rolling it onto the tarp. Once on the tarp they hefted it up and dropped it into the wheelbarrow.

"You really think they are going to get back up—even after we put 'em down again?"

"Why not?"

Walter walked behind Jeff as he pushed the wheelbarrow forward, the dead thing's arm dangling off the side and its feet nearly scraping the ground, bouncing with each step Jeff took.

"I don't know, I just figured once you shoot them in the head— that's it, they're dead again, you know?"

"If that's it, then fine, you won't hear me complain. But I've been watching them a lot. I didn't want to say anything around the others, but sometimes I see them raising up their arms again, grabbing at the air."

"Are you serious?"

"I wouldn't yank ya on this. What if destroying their brain only kept them down for a while—long enough for whatever is making 'em come back to figure out another way of making the body get up and attack us? Here's good enough. Dump that thing."

Jeff emptied the wheelbarrow, the dead thing tumbling out and falling like a rag doll to the earth. Walter pulled the tarp from the dead thing and followed Jeff back for the next one.

"I guess it's possible. Maybe we should strike the heart too?"

"I dunno. Might work. Might not. My thinking is that however these dead things are getting upright again it's affecting the whole body so I think the only way to really get rid of them is to burn them up. Just look at them, it's like they want to get back up. Like whatever is in there is looking for a way to get the whole body up and running."

Jeff didn't know what else to say, in truth he didn't want to think about it anymore. He just wanted to get today's tasks finished so he could make his family a touch safer.

"Let's get this sad sack."

They hefted the twitching deader onto the wheelbarrow, walked it back to its friend and dumped it out. One body became two, and after a few more trips the pile was starting to grow. After an hour or so Barbara came out to join them and by then they were halfway done piling up the bodies.

The two deaders that Jeff had noticed in the distance were now close enough to be of concern. Jeff and Barbara walked over to them, each drawing one in the opposite direction. Jeff went for the knees with the shovel and dropped it instantly. Barbara went for the temple with the crowbar, puncturing the side of its head with one vicious blow. As the dead thing dropped Jeff brought the shovel down onto the deaders neck and then applied his weight atop the shovel till he could hear the spinal column crack. Barbara pulled out her crowbar and kicked the deader to the ground. She punctured its head several more times till it stopped trying to get up.

"Someone's getting good at this."

"It's still friggin' gross."

"If you two are done playing, maybe we could get back to work?"

32 LIKE A GRAVEYARD

Everyone huddled around in a circle near the back of the SUV. They were scooping out the last bites of food in their respective cans. Eddie tilted back a can of creamed corn and let the cool salty sweet food glide down his gullet. He was trying not to gag on it as he swallowed. Though he knew he needed the food in his gut to keep him going strong it was still a challenge to eat anything right out of the can. He detested it, as did the others, and wished that cars had microwave ovens instead of glove boxes, but they didn't so he tilted the can back and finished it off.

He let the can clang to the ground where it bounced and rolled over to the rest of the discarded cans.

"Everyone ready?" Scott called out.

More cans clanged to the ground.

One of the children burped, causing the others to giggle.

"Let's roll. Hopefully we'll still have daylight by the time we get there," Eddie said, slinging a backpack over his shoulder and picking up a tire-iron.

Frankie and Joseph followed behind them.

"Abdul, Chuck, Chung-Hee, you guys want to take the rear and make sure no one falls behind?"

Chung-Hee looked to the others. They nodded in acceptance and Chung-Hee spoke for them all, "You got it."

"Everyone else keep up. Eyes open and mouths shut, please."

"Kids, if any of you get tired let one of us know. You can sit on someone's shoulders for a bit, okay?"

"Okay," Yussef said. "We're going to be strong, okay."

"Sounds good, kiddo. Keep up that attitude," Scott said as he and Judy started moving forward.

Alexis allowed the kids to move forward first and then she stuck right behind them, already looking around wearily.

Janice watched her as the children moved closer to them and then she grabbed Alexis' shoulder. She stared her in the eyes, "I'll do what I can to help you with the children. You're doing so good with them."

She smiled, "Thanks. I...could use the help." Alexis couldn't recall hearing Janice's voice before, if she had she knew it couldn't have been with the strength her tone conveyed. Even the woman looking her in the eyes didn't seem like the same person she'd been traveling with. This was the first time she looked alive and not just breathing.

Carrie still clutched the keys in her hand. She didn't want to get out and join them, but she didn't want to be alone. Begrudgingly she had joined them while they were eating, all the while voicing her opinion on how stupid everyone was for going along with this. After not gaining any traction with her complaints she filled her mouth with a can of cool Clam Chowder. She complained about the soup too, but kept eating it anyway.

Eddie led the way up the road through the lines of traffic. Each car held the potential for danger and there were a lot of cars on the road. Many of them were smeared with blood—handprints and blood spatters as common as mud flaps and spoilers. Glass shards and dried pools of blood that were now no more than washed out stains on the roadway became mile markers.

After only a few minutes of walking up the road the fear of a deader being in them was replaced by the fear of nothing being in them. Eddie was struck by the realization that he was essentially walking through a graveyard. Aside from their footfalls and the gentle breeze it was as quiet as a graveyard too.

"I wonder what happened to all these people," Joseph said.

"They either survived or didn't."

"No shit, Frank."

"Some of them probably got away."

"I hope so."

"Let's not worry about them. Let's worry about ourselves," Eddie said, hoping to steer their minds off of the very same things he was thinking. It was a dark train of thought. He could picture in his mind's eye how these people met their ends.

Eddie figured they were just sitting in traffic. The first few days no one really knew what was happening. The media was as confused as the people listening and by the time anyone knew how serious a situation they were in, it was too late.

He could see a family trying to get home. A wife trying to get to her husband. A young man going for a job interview. Eddie passed a shattered window and pictured a woman being dragged out by her hair, kicking and screaming while someone rushed to help her only to be bitten or scratched and end up the same way. Eddie could see it happening like a domino effect. He thought about what he would've done had he not known all he knew now. He'd probably try helping someone in the same scenario he played out in his head only to meet the same fate.

"I'm tired," Stacey called out.
"And now it starts," Scott said, turning to his wife.
"Scott, can I sit on your shoulders?"
"Okay, but only for a few minutes."
"Okay," Stacey smiled.

After Scott lifted her onto his shoulders the other kids instantly became just as tired of walking. Jon-Jon, Abdul, and Joseph joined Scott in sacrificing their shoulders.

For a moment they all had smiles on their faces. For a moment they forgot that they weren't parentless. They were high in the air smiling as the last hours of daylight made the sky look like a melted Popsicle. They forgot about never seeing their mommies. They forgot about daddy never coming home. They forgot about home entirely.

Then Yussef pointed at a deader walking towards them and they forgot they were having a good time.

33 YARD WORK IS HARD WORK

All the bodies near the house were piled atop one another. It was a disgusting mass of twitching limbs.

"I can't believe we had this many bodies around the house."

"Believe it. Let's go get some of these branches laying all over the place and then let's light 'em up."

"Do you think the fire will draw more of them here?"

"The thought has crossed my mind."

"What will we do?"

"Just what we've been doing."

"What if it's a lot?"

"Doesn't change anything. We have our contingencies. We've talked about all this before."

They threw fallen branches onto the pile and then Jeff started to douse the bodies in gasoline. He circled around a few times till the container was empty. Then Walter made a torch with a piece of branch and a rag dipped in gas and walked around igniting the gasoline.

First the clothing started to burn and then, so did the rotting flesh. The flames seemed to move slowly but within minutes the pile of bodies was a raging bonfire. The smell was obscenely revolting, and yet a pleasing scent reminiscent of honey-glazed ham was intermingled.

"I'm getting kinda hungry. Let's go see if your mom is cooking anything up."

"How the hell are you hungry?"

"How are you not? This was some hard work."

"Gross dad."

By the time the three of them entered the house and cleaned up, Laura and Maria had put together a lunch for the kids. Which consisted of jelly bread sandwiches, watered down juices, and the last of the applesauce.

They ate quickly and scampered off to play, as Walter, Jeff, and Barbara took a seat at the table.

"You three look exhausted already."

"That's not nice, ma, dad always looks like this."

"Funny. Dear, please tell me we have something other than jelly sandwiches for lunch today?"

"Well, you kids can have peanut butter and jelly. And I'll even make you all triple-deckers if you want."

"Yes please," Jeff said with a smile.

"Only if you cut mine into squares."

Walter only grumbled, and Laura smiled as a result.

"It's not just kid-food, Walter, it'll do you good on these hard days. It has a lot of calories, a lot of fat, and a lot of protein."

"So does a hoagie."

"Well, when you go back out, swing by the deli and pick up some cold cuts."

"Are you done for today?"

"Yeah, I think so. I can't do anymore. I thought it best if we all wash up today. Empty out the open containers of water and replenish them with fresh water. See if we can store any more if we have any more empty bottles or anything."

"And tomorrow?"

"Tomorrow we're going to hit a few more homes. Run over to Gupp's and look for fencing. Hopefully we can start putting up some kind of fence tomorrow 'round this time."

"Yeah, then we can start taking the kids out regularly."

"That'd be nice."

"For a bit at least. I for one cannot wait until winter. The colder the better. The more snow the better. Slow them things down."

"It'll slow us down too. But snow is a long ways off."

"You never know. Anyhoo, we'll just worry about the fence for now. Just keep doing one thing at a time and try to make ourselves better off for the next day, and the next day, and the day after that."

Laura cut each sandwich down the middle from corner to corner and slid a plate over to each of them.

"Thanks mom."

"Ditto."

Grumble.

"Oh, Walter," Laura smiled.

Then she tilted her head and looked out the window at the large bonfire blazing in the front of the house.

"Makes me think of some of your war stories."

"It feels like a war."

Jeff and Barbara kept their mouths quiet and full. Their father rarely ever spoke of his time at war, not that he wasn't proud of his service, he was, but he related talking about it to the feeling of pulling scabs off of wounds. It was an itchy, raw feeling and was best left alone.

Walter much preferred to talk about tomorrow. He didn't have a lot of use for yesterdays, and he sure didn't want to waste today talking about them. His children knew this; Laura did too, perhaps more than anyone. So when Walter mentioned the war, even in brief, they kept quiet in the hopes that more talk of his time in it would be revealed.

But he had nothing more to say about it, as usual.

Laura watched the fire and the room was full of chewing and an occasional grumble. The sounds of the kids playing was a faint noise in the background.

34 THE BRIDGE

The dead man was wearing a necktie and nothing else. His body was shredded as if a hundred hands had clawed at his body trying to rip his insides out. His bottom ribs were exposed and what intestines he had left were draped over his genitals. His nose was bitten off and his eyes were gone, replaced by two ragged holes. He opened his mouth and a throaty gurgle poured forth.

Frankie, gripping a pry-bar, stormed over to the dead thing and swung violently at the dead mans head, sending him into a car and then sliding down. Frankie kicked it as it tried to get back up and swung again into the dead mans face. He swung again and again till his face resembled a jack-o-lantern that'd been kicked in and left on the porch far too long.

The group continued forward, unimpeded by the violence. Frankie rejoined them once he caught his breath, looking around like a wild animal for another dead thing to pulverize. Frankie loved the adrenaline rush. It was the only time he didn't feel run down and tired. It made him feel alive, strong, and he wanted to stay that way.

"There's the bridge," Scott pointed.

"We're making okay time," Judy added, "Still got daylight too."

"Not for long," Eddie said.

"No, but hopefully long enough to light our way across the bridge."

"In a perfect world."

"How's everybody looking back there?"

"The kids are still riding high. They're probably putting a hurting on the fellas' backs."

"I'll swap someone out," Joseph offered, and then fell back and did just that.

"Stacey? You want to ride on my shoulders for a bit? I think Scott is getting tired."

"Are you getting tired?"

Scott chuckled, "Yes, Stacey, I'm getting a bit tired. Uncle Scott could use a break, whattya say?"

"Okay. You can take a break."

They moved over to the side for a moment and switched off.

"Thanks Eddie."

"Don't mention it."

Eddie couldn't help but think of his little sister as Stacey sat atop his shoulders. It took everything in him to not break down and cry. He searched the roadway and hoped to see a deader or two, anything to get this kid off his back and his mind off of his dead siblings. The memories were far too painful. If he could bury them all in the dirt and walkaway he would. He'd love to forget it all and wander around without knowing whom he was or where he'd come from. Dead family, dead friends, and a dying world were the things you needed amnesia to forget.

The daylight was being dragged down across the horizon and the sky was cooling in color and temperature. As the group made their way through the rows of abandoned vehicles the shadows grew longer and deeper. The air grew chillier, but not by much, just enough to cool the sweat off the backs of everyone walking.

Judy found herself in the lead and was walking quicker and quicker. Scott and Judy used to walk for an hour or more every morning. Judy loved hiking, and walking. She wasn't an outdoorsy kind of woman and she wasn't super concerned about staying in shape she just liked to walk. It always made her feel better. Early in their relationship Scott tagged along on her walks just to spend time with her, but after awhile he appreciated it in equal measure.

Her years of walking came in very useful nowadays and she felt herself gaining energy from walking whereas the others just grew tired. She had to make an effort to keep her pace in line with the others but it was getting harder the closer they grew to the bridge. Her and Scott were now a few car lengths ahead of everyone else and the bridge felt like a beacon of hope as opposed to the act of disparity it had been made out to be.

Frankie dropped back from the group and hung around the tail end, making small talk with Chuck and Chung-Hee before falling behind them as well. He lingered around the cars now, taking longer and longer to get through them. The blood smears started to look like letters. It was a language Frankie wanted to learn. Some of the smears and spatters looked like paintings in a modern art exhibit and he even started touching the dried smears as he went by. Following them as if they were his. He looked drunk, uninhibited as he continued. Chung-Hee looked back to see where he was and at a quick glance it only looked as if Frankie were running his hands along the cars as you would a wall just to feel the texture.

Frankie caught back up with the tail end of the group and as he did a few deaders presented themselves. One crawling out from underneath a truck, another getting up from the side of the road, and another falling over the concrete divider. Frankie smiled and walked over to one of them, pry-bar at the ready.

Chung-Hee went after one, and Chuck the other.

Chuck was still very much squeamish about fighting the dead off. He kept his distance and hated having to get close at all to them. Regardless he got in and dispatched the dead thing, as did Chung-Hee who saw it simply as a task. He went about killing the dead as he did taking out the garbage. He just went and got it done. There was no joy in it, or trepidation. He just did it.

Frankie on the other hand was still hitting the thing in the head. The body bouncing from the force of each blow. As Frankie walked away the body continued to convulse and twitch.

It was near dark now. The group had made it to the foot of the bridge. The tollbooths were clogged with cars, trucks, and buses. The scene before them was an absolute nightmare, and the bridge beyond it looked only slightly better.

Scott turned to the group, "Any of you ever see the movie The Gauntlet, with Clint Eastwood?"

"Yeah," Jon-Jon said, "but didn't he at least have a fucking bus?"

35 STOCKPILING

With little trouble the next day came and so did the next day's tasks. Walter, Jeff, and Barbara were up and ready to go by the time the rest of the household trickled down the stairs. Jeff hugged and kissed his little ones goodbye. They were upset with him for leaving, and as much as it tore him open he knew he had to go out so that they could have a better tomorrow. Or at least the chance of one. He gave his wife a kiss, and Walter did the same. They were both told to be safe and Barbara stood around awkwardly just wanting to leave already and get it over with.

"We ready?"

Walter nodded, "Yep, let's get on with it."

"Are you coming back for lunch?"

"I don't know, we'll be gone however long it takes. So don't count on it I guess."

"Daddy, I want to come too. I can help," Tommy said, standing tall.

"Oh, Tommy-boy, I know you can help me, but I need you here. You have to look after your little brother and sister," then Jeff got down on his knee and leaned in close to whisper, "and you have to keep grandma, and mommy safe too. They're old ladies."

Tommy thought about this for a second. His mom and grandma were old, he thought. And Sandra and Wally were too little to help out, "Okay. I'll stay and protect them."

Tommy raised his chin proudly, smiling at his father.

They drove off to the last house they had scavenged the other day and picked up where they left off. There was a lonely deader staggering a few feet down the street. Initially it was walking in the other direction, but upon hearing their arrival it had turned around and started walking towards them.

"I got it," Jeff said, walking towards it briskly.

He quickly dispatched the dead thing and left it to twitch in the street.

They hit the few homes on the street, yielding plenty of supplies with each one. They had even scored a few weapons as well: a shotgun, and three handguns, each with a few boxes of ammunition. Whomever they belonged to was obviously trying to prepare for the deaders as they were sitting loaded at a small kitchen table, loaded and ready to fire. Also on the table was a radio and flashlight, which they took as well.

"Building up our arsenal," Walter smiled as he put them in the back of the truck.

"Not a bad haul."

"Gupp's?"

Jeff nodded and took a turn behind the wheel. Driving off to the Gupp's Hardware, the local store that Walter and his son routinely visited almost every weekend during the spring for one thing or another.

"Going house to house I kind of hoped we'd run into someone."

"Anyone in particular?"

"No. Just anyone alive, ya know, surely there has to be more of us left in town."

"I've been thinking about that too. I'm sure there has to be, but there were a lot of them things that came through town."

"Maybe we should drive around looking for others?"

"Maybe, kiddo, maybe. Let's go to Gupp's first though, see if we can't scrounge up some fencing materials."

"Where would we start, though? If we were going to look for others?"

"I'd want to hit the police station first. I think that's where most people would still try to go to for help, and Davis was organizing everyone from there if any of his people are left I'd think they would still operate out of there."

"Worst case, maybe we can find some more guns, too."

"Well, here we are."

"The police station is right down the street. Should we go check it out first?"

"Let's stay on task, okay. Once we finish up here we can head over there later. Look at this…it's nice and boarded up. Looks just the way they left it."

They walked around the building, making sure no deaders were in the area, and came back around to the front entrance.

"I sure do hate doing this," Walter said, before he smashed out the glass on the front door.

"No alarm."

"They had a silent alarm. I remember they switched it out, because the old one would always get tripped on accident, and the damned thing was blaring. He just got fed up and upgraded his system."

Walter reached in and spun the lock, opening the door. He didn't think a deader would be in the store, but he entered cautiously all the same. Barbara followed and Jeff hung back momentarily, making sure they wouldn't be followed in by anyone, or anything.

"All right," Jeff said, catching up with them, "they have what we want?"

"Not sure, but take a few of these snow shovels back to the truck will ya?"

"Snow shovels. Really?"

"Hopefully we'll be able to use them, no?"

"Yeah. I guess I hope so."

Walter looked around. The place was nearly empty. Practically wiped clean. All the practical things that one might think to acquire while in an emergency were gone; batteries, flashlights, gas cans, extension cords, etc. Thinking outside of the box, Walter looked at a pallet of spring seed mix. Why would anyone have wanted to grab these earlier? Walter saw they could be used like sandbags.

He spun around. Noting the shovels, rakes, hoes, and then noticed a few post diggers, "Barbara, go bring those out to Jeff."

She bundled them up in her arms and carried them out.

There was no lumber left in the store, but Walter spotted several bags of QuickCrete and figured they'd be good for something eventually--at least for setting the posts. As soon as his kids came back he had them carry those out as well.

By the time they were ready to head home they had found some machetes, scores of nails and screws, random tools, chainsaws, toilet paper from the backroom, cases of soda for the small vending machine near the register. Surprisingly the hodgepodge of goods took up the bed of the truck. Walter wanted to come back for the pallet of seed mix, but found he had to explain for what.

"You really want us to come back for seed mix?"

"Think of them as sandbags."

"Okay, but for what?"

"For fortification, what else?"

"With no fence, what do we fortify?"

"Whatever we need to. Besides, just because we didn't find what we need here doesn't mean we abort the fence. There's more than one way to skin a cat."

"We're not skinning cats."

"We can fortify the door, the porch--What will it hurt to come back for it?"

"Our backs, and our gas tank."

"Then I'll come back myself for it."

"Fine. Fine, we'll come back for it. Now let's go bring this shit home, okay?"

***

Only a block away from Walter and his kids Davis stared down at the floor of the holding cell.

I'm not going to die in here. I'm not going to die in here.

This was his mantra. He would not accept this place as his last. He knew he would get out eventually. If only he could convince the others, who already looked as if they'd resigned themselves to death.

"Why is this happening?" Danni asked.

"Just stop it, okay?" Keith said, growing angry with the young woman. "It's not fucking fair, we get it. We know it. Just deal with it okay?"

"Someone will come looking for us," Davis said, "there has to be someone left. There has to be..."

143

36 THROUGH THE WRECKAGE

"Okay, kids," Scott said, "This is the part where you need to be big and strong, okay? We need you to stick together and stay close. Don't go running off, don't touch anything, understand?"

They nodded in unison. They understood the drill, or at least the speech, but listening and doing what they were asked of were usually very different things.

Alexis took Stacey by the hand. Janice held Yussef's. Abdul kept Chris on his shoulders. Judy, Dawn, and Jon-Jon agreed to look after Leela and Nick. Jon-Jon walked behind them while Judy took Nick's hand, and Dawn took Leela's. In Leela's other hand she still clung to her small stuffed lion.

Chuck and Chung-Hee continued to stay at the tail end of the group, while Frankie, Eddie, and Joseph led them forward.

"Hang back a little," Eddie called back as they approached the tollbooths.

The three of them walked forward cautiously, observing every open door and blood trail on the way to the cash only lane. The windows of the booths were all smeared in blood and the waning sunlight made it look like liquid rust.

Frankie stepped ahead in eager fashion, hoping to find something to hit. Eddie stuck close, but knew it best to stay two steps behind and make sure there weren't any surprises to be had by speeding up.

They were now at the coin toss and all was quiet. The amount of abandoned cars was staggering and the scene before them was surreal and disconcerting. It reminded them of how quickly the world turned to shit in those first few days. Walking through the aftermath painted a detailed picture for them. A picture so clear they could almost hear the screams and cries of panic and pain twisting and crashing and burning like so much rubber and steel on the blood soaked asphalt.

Joseph waived the group to come forward—Abdul led them, being careful to check his surroundings as he moved, but not so much to jostle and make nauseous his little human passenger, Chris. The tiny blond haired boy had been through so much that he appeared more like a ghost than a child. A wafer-thin boy with the haunted eyes of and old dying man. He'd gotten carsick a time or two, and didn't do to well while eating straight from the can, so the last thing Abdul wanted was for the boy to vomit all over the both of them.

As the rest of the group started moving along, Frankie, Eddie, and Joseph moved forward once again. The bridge almost immediately began to incline.

"My legs are going to be jelly by the time we get over this bitch."

"Yeah man, I can already feel it. Maybe we can just roll down the other side?"

"Guys," Scott called over, "What about the boats? Can we see anything from here?" Scott asked as he hurried over to the side of the bridge.

"Let's look."

"Damn. They're pretty far away," Joseph noted.

"I figured they would've been closer."

"Not at all. Shit."

"It looks like it would take us just as much time to get to one of them as it would to cross this thing."

As the rest of the group caught up, Jon-Jon picked up on what they were talking about and joined in, "I know the Tarrytown Marina isn't that far once we cross over. But we'd be moving northwest to get there and that would take us away from Connetiticut."

"It might be worth it. We can move faster on the water. We would have to go southeast around Manhattan and Long Island and then back up."

Frankie started walking away, "First we gotta get over this fucking thing, right? So let's get it over with."

Eddie started moving as well, "Jon, can we see the marina from the other side of the bridge?"

"Not sure. If we can during the day, doesn't mean it'll be visible by the time we cross over either."

"Yeah, daylights burning up fast. Let's get going then."

Frankie, Eddie, and Joseph took the lead once again, trying to move fast up the bridge while they still had sunlight.

"You hear that?"

"Yeah," Eddie turned to the group, holding up his hand for them to wait.

They kept moving, the sound getting louder.

Skkkkurrrrtch.

Skkkkurrrrrrrtch.

Skkkkuuuuurrrrrrrtch.

Frankie held the pry-bar out to his side, half cocked and ready to swing. Eddie pulled a bat from his backpack and held it with both hands. Joseph stood at the ready with a tire iron, positioning himself to be able to move quickly in any direction.

Skkkkuuuuurrrrrrrtch.

The sound was upon them, but they couldn't see anything. Eddie looked around inside the cars—nothing. Joseph could see nothing over them either.

"I can smell the fucker, but where is it?"

As Frankie asked the question something grabbed his ankle and pulled.

"Fuck!"

Frankie tugged away, but the slithering upper half of what was once a very heavy woman didn't let go. Frankie fell to the ground. Eddie ran to him, tire iron held high, and smashed it into the woman's head, smashing her face into the street.

She was wedged in between and underneath two cars that were bumper to bumper. Her intestines trailed behind her and there was no sight of her lower half. Yellow chunks of fatty tissue decorated the street around her and behind her.

Eddie hit her again as Frankie pulled his foot away. Joseph helped him get to his feet.

"One of your old girlfriends?"

"What can I say? I like 'em big."

Joseph smiled and patted off his back.

"She fucking stinks. Either of you hear anything else?"

They paused, listening.

"Nothing."

Eddie waived them forward and the three of them continued to lead the way through the wreckage.

37 ENDURANCE TEST

Abdul was starting to sweat now. The incline of the bridge coupled with the additional forty or so pounds on his shoulders was starting to take its toll, but Abdul refused to give in to his weakness. He would push on and block out the urge to slow down or take Chris off his shoulders. He would endure, and in the end he and Chris, and even the others would be better for it. If Abdul didn't carry the burden, someone else would have to. That was weakness. Abdul wasn't weak.

"Close your eyes," he told Chris as he approached the dead whale of a woman.

Chris cupped his hands around his eyes.

"Can I open them now?"

"Yes, but keep looking ahead."

Scott held Judy's hand and she gripped it back fiercely, "How you doing?"

"Okay," she said. "Just absolutely terrified."

"We're doing good. Just stay positive."

"I don't want to die on this bridge. Remember when I was working in Manhattan?"

"Of course."

"Well, I never really said anything then, but I was always afraid I'd die on my commute. It seemed like everyday there was an accident. Not usually fatal, but you know, with my anxiety I always thought it would be my turn."

"I thought you liked commuting."

"I hated it. The only thing I liked was being able to read on the bus, but half the time I just stared out the window biting my nails."

"Well, you don't work in the city anymore and we're not going to die on this bridge, if anything I'll throw you over the side and you can drown in the Hudson."

"Already considered it. Suicide fencing."

"Shit, I didn't even notice that. Looks like we could climb it though."

"What the hell are you guys talking about?"

"Double suicide. Want in?"

"Are you fucking serious?"

"No, actually if you jumped with us, it would be a triple."

Jon-Jon stared at them disbelievingly.

"We're not considering it. Relax, we just noticed the fencing—in case, you know, we had to jump."

"There's something wrong with you two."

"We know," Judy smiled.

"Hey, what do you think the cause of death was with the fat lady?"

"In my expert opinion, I think she ran faster than she ever did in her life, and when she stopped, her upper half had gained so much momentum that it kept going. Essentially she ripped herself in half."

"See what I mean? You're twisted."

"No, what's twisted is that we still have yet to see her legs."

Before the group had realized it, the fading sunlight was gone. The sky was black and blue once again, but pierced with the pinpricks of starlight, grey clouds, and the thick sliver of moon that sat in the sky, shimmering on the water.

It didn't fully register till they were at the peak of the bridge, when the rest of their journey would be shrouded in darkness and slashed by deep obsidian shadows. There were no beacons of light. No streetlights in the distance. No lit buildings. Just darkness and dim moonlit forms.

"Let's be careful," Eddie said as he began to walk down the decline.

"Legs like jelly yet?"

"Not too bad, you?"

"Starting to feel it. I'll probably collapse as soon as we can."

"No shit. How you holding up Frank?"

"I'm jelly. Feel like my legs are wobbling."

"Want to take a break?"

"Fuck no. We need to get off this bridge as soon as possible. The longer it takes us the longer we're putting ourselves at a huge risk."

Eddie understood. He didn't want to take a break either, but if people needed to catch their breath while there was a moment to do it, he saw no reason not to oblige them.

Alexis turned to Stacey, "You okay, little lady?"

Stacey looked at her with wide terrified eyes, "I'm scared."

"Me too, but we've gone through worse, right? Just hang in there. We're almost done. Then maybe we can get on a boat. Wouldn't that be cool?"

"I don't know how to swim."

"We don't need to swim. See Chuck over there. He knows how to drive a boat, so all we have to do is find one."

"Okay."

Alexis and Dawn shared a look. They were both as scared as Stacey, but they knew they had to be strong for them. Janice walked with a renewed vigor. Her maternal instincts took over and she walked with Yussef, making him feel safe in her company. She let him know she was there for him and would protect him. As much as it hurt her heart to hold a child's hand that wasn't hers she held firm and kept repeating to herself that she'd want someone else to safeguard her children had she lost her life and not theirs.

The world had become a scary place. Scary for adults, scary for children. Jon-Jon couldn't decide who had more to fear. He felt that at least the children were too young to really grasp the entirety of the situation. Being a child and having no parents, essentially being raised on the road by a group of strangers was an awful way to live. Realizing that humanity was on the brink of extinction, however, was an entirely different kind of awful. One that made him think if any of this even mattered.

Cancer killed his mother and father. She fought it till the bitter end. His father tried to kill himself slowly with alcohol after that, and when he was diagnosed himself many years after his wife died, he fully gave himself over to it and longed for its final embrace. He'd given some consideration as to what he would do had he ever have to face the same demon—fight like his mother, or go quietly like his father. In the end it didn't matter. Not in any way that Jon could see. *How was this world not like cancer?*

38 THE CELL

"What time is it?"

"You don't want to know," Keith said.

"How long has it been?"

"We've been in here at least two days, now," Davis noted.

"It doesn't look like any of them have lost interest," Topher said, as he looked about the room.

"I think I'm losing my fucking mind. They just keep looking at us, reaching for us…"

"Easy Keith, it's better if you don't look at them," Davis suggested, keeping his eyes toward the ground.

"How can you not?"

"Just stare at the floor."

"Oh, and the smell, and the sounds will just go away? How about the fact that we're all going to fucking die in here? How about that Bruce?"

"There is nothing we can do about that now is there? What we can do is try to stay calm, and bide our time. Hope that someone will find us…that something will get the attention of these friggin' things and maybe we'll get out of here."

"You're asking for a lot of hope."

"That I am, but if we don't stay calm we'll just end up killing ourselves in here."

Clem looked at Davis, "Sheriff, if it came to that, do you…do you have enough bullets for all of us."

"Clem…no…"

"It's okay. I'm good with dying. Here is just as good as anywhere else. My soul will go on.

"Old timer, if you're asking me what I think you're asking me, I just don't know if I could."

"I'd do it. I'll do it for any of you," Keith said.

"Well, this conversation just got about as dark as it could get. Tell you the truth I thought about offing myself early on, before you found me Mr. Sheriff," Topher said, recalling his days squirrelled away in his musky Control Room.

"I think we can stop calling me Sheriff, now."

"Okay, Bruce. Well, the only reason I didn't do it was because what was the rush? It looked like my days were numbered anyway. So I just kind of hung out, made my piece with dying and now I'm here—making piece with it all over again."

"So what the hell are you saying?"

"What I'm saying is you can put that gun up to your chin and pull the trigger, or you can sit back and think about some of the good things you've had in your life and let whatever happens happen. Just let it go, if you die you die, but what's the rush?"

"What's the rush? Look around you?"

"Don't look around. Think about a good moment, a good memory--"

"That's enough just shut the fuck up already."

"Keith, please."

"Topher, I'll give it a shot," Clem said.

Too afraid to say any more Topher simply nodded at Clem and then closed his eyes. He pictured himself sitting by a fire drinking a hot chocolate. His ex-wife was sitting on his lap. She was sorry for being such a bitch.

Clem closed his eyes and thought of Lorraine.

Davis, Danni, and Keith looked around the cell. Cement walls on two sides, bars on the other, with the dead desperately trying to grasp at them from the other side with no loss of vigor and no lack of effort.

Danni tried to close her eyes and think of something good, but everything she thought about just made her hurt more.

Bruce turned to Keith, "Want to go fishing tomorrow?"

Keith smiled and closed his eyes. The water was still. Cold beers were in the cooler. The fish were biting.

39 DON'T LOOK IN THE CAR

There was a patch on the bridge where it looked like all the vehicles tried to move to one side of the lane and as the group took advantage of this opening by moving quickly through it, they found out why the vehicles were pushed over. An ambulance was in the distance; it's reflective surfaces standing out in the moonlight. Its back doors were open and the front of it was smashed into another vehicle.

Frankie led them to the ambulance. They slowed on approaching it to examine the interior and after seeing the gurney covered in dried blood they moved away. The ambulance had caused such a jam that the group had to climb over a car in order to continue moving.

The bridge grew congested. The cars and trucks were inches apart, many bumper to bumper, and others adorned with damage from ramming into each other.

There were noises in the distance that sounded like gunfire. Single shots with a steady pace, like someone with a rifle.

"Think that's a sniper?" Jon asked.

"Could be. Could be a hunter."

"I can't tell where it's coming from."

"Could be anywhere."

"Maybe it's good for us, if someone is shooting, don't you think?"

"I was just thinking that. If anything is nearby, maybe the sounds would draw attention away from us."

Frankie ran his fingers along the cars. Feeling the cool steel on his fingertips.

Thump.

Frankie jumped.

"What? What is it?"

Thump.

"A noise…"

Thump.

Joseph signaled for the others to hold up. Eddie and Frankie tried to pinpoint the sound. It was coming from inside one of the cars.

"There's got to be one of them trapped inside a car."

"Poor bastard."

"Fuck them."

Thump.

"There. It's got to be one of these."

Thump.

Frankie peered into a car.

Thump.

He had the right car. He could hear the thumping as clear as day, but he didn't see anything. It was dark inside, and the windows were smeared with blood and grime.

Thump.

"See anything?"

He did. His eyes found what was making the sound and he wished he didn't. He wished they never even gave it a thought. "Wish I didn't man. Don't look--"

Too late. Eddie began to wretch, throwing up the canned food he fought so hard to gulp down to begin with. It was warmer going out than it was going in.

"Fuck man. That's horrible. That's so fucking horrible," he said, wiping the spit from his lip.

Thump.

Thump.

Thump.

"We can't leave that."

"I'm not opening the door. I can't look again."

"We don't have a gun, Ed, and I can't go in there."

"Let's set the car on fire."

"Got a rag?"

"Yeah, I have a spare shirt."

"Joe. Get everyone away. Get a few cars down."

"You got it. Everything cool?"

"Far from it. We're going to take care of it, but don't come over here—trust me. Gonna set the car on fire."

"You think that's a good idea?"

"No. But if you saw this, I think you'd agree that we can't leave it alone."

"Fair enough dude."

With that Joseph and Scott led the way. Avoiding the car and getting the others further down the bridge.

Eddie tore a strip of cloth from a spare shirt in his backpack. Frankie pulled out a lighter and a small can of lighter fluid, which had come in very handy since the world nearly came to a screeching halt.

Frankie soaked the cloth with the lighter fluid and jimmied open the gas door with the pry-bar. Once the gas cap was off Frankie shoved in the cloth and forced it down with his finger till there was only a small strip hanging out.

"Let me do it," Eddie offered, "you're hands are soaked in that shit."

"Go right ahead." Frankie tossed him the lighter.

Eddie snatched it out of the air. Frankie and Joseph walked away towards the rest of the group.

Thump.

Eddie flicked the lighter. The rag lit with ease and the flame crawled inside the gas tank. Eddie ran away expecting the car to explode behind him, but it didn't.

The group watched in anticipation—moments passed and the car still didn't explode. Flames grew from underneath the vehicle, and it was smoking, but far from what they had expected.

"Why isn't it blowing up?"

"I'm thinking when it happened to Gerty that it was a fluke. Everyone always says only cars blow up on TV."

"Yeah, but shouldn't it be a bigger fire though?"

"It's building, you can see that."

"Yeah, man, it's doing the trick. The whole thing will burn out soon enough."

"Fuck it, let's get out of here."

"The quicker the better. The bigger that fire gets the more things will be drawn to it."

40 A FAMILIAR ODOR

The night continued to grow cool, allowing it's darkness to seem all the more sinister and it's shadows all the more deeper. Though they had nearly made it to the end of the bridge the light from the car fire burned bright.

Chris had fallen asleep on Abdul's shoulders. He slid one way and then the other as Abdul continued to walk. His back and neck ached furiously. His legs burned and his arms kept falling asleep. He wanted to drop to the ground and just give up, but he pushed on.

The abandoned vehicles on the bridge continued to tell a story. Cars were smashed into the sides. Trucks were left rammed into the back of other vehicles. Windows were smashed in, windshields kicked out, doors left ajar. Police cars were stuck in between lanes, unable to weave through traffic. A bus in the distance lay on its side.

Frankie climbed on top of a car. Standing on the roof of the sedan he peered forward into the dark distance.

"Anything?"

"Don't see shit."

"How much further?"

"Almost there. Maybe another ten minutes. Twenty tops."

Frankie jumped down and they continued to move down the tight twisting lanes of wreckage.

As they passed the bus, Chung-Hee could hear a scratching noise.

"Guys?"

Chuck turned, hearing it too, followed by excited grunts. Several deaders clawed their way out of the bus, knocking aside one of it's emergency exit windows.

"Oh, fuck. Guys!"

The group halted. Frankie and Eddie jumped on top of a car to see past everyone and to make eye contact with Chung-Hee.

"What is it?"

"Don't stop, keep moving," Chung-Hee pleaded, "We got company."

"Joe, lead everyone down the bridge quick."

Joseph didn't want to lead the group away from the action, he wanted to stay and fight alongside his brother. Had his mother not been among the group he would've sent them on their way alone and stayed by his brother's side. Instead he simply nodded and kept moving.

Scott stood aside, "Eddie, we can just out walk them. There's no need to stay back and take them down."

"We're not going to take them down. You're right. But we're still going to make sure everyone gets some distance, and that those fuckers aren't right on our asses."

"Okay man, just be careful."

Scott caught up with Judy and Frankie, Eddie, Chung-Hee and Chuck hung back to deal with the deaders.

"You got any of that shirt left?"

"Yeah, what do you got in mind?"

"I say we start some more car fires."

"Sounds like a plan."

Eddie dug through his bag and dug out the shredded shirt. He ripped into two pieces and tossed one to Frankie.

Chung-Hee opened a nearby car to check the gas gauge. The tank was more than halfway full.

"This one looks good."

"Pop the tank."

"Guys, they're getting closer."

"Moving pretty quick for deaders."

"Yeah, they must be hungry."

Chung-Hee popped the gas tank as Frankie doused the rag in lighter fluid. After he was done shoving it in Eddie lit the rag. They moved back a few more cars and did the same thing. Both cars were slow to burn but the time the deaders neared them they had flames licking up from underneath the chassis and from out of the open doors and cracked windows.

"That oughtta slow 'em down."

"Come on, let's catch up with the others."

They jogged over to the others. Eddie and Frankie returning to lead the pack and Chuck and Chung-Hee in the back.

"We'll keep an eye on them," Chuck said. "Just get us off this bridge like now."

"We're almost there, man."

The deaders had no choice but to continue walking through the flames from the blazing cars. They didn't hesitate or flinch, but as they moved slowly through the flames that lapped at them their skin singed and burned. Small blotches of skin and cloth caught fire, but as they continued forward the flames died off.

"Dude, do you…"

"Shh. Just keep fucking moving. Don't even say it."

"You can smell it, right?"

"Just keep moving man. Quickly."

"Fuck dude. It reeks."

"I know, I know."

"I knew this was a shit idea."

"Don't fuckin' start Frankie, we're right at the end."

Scott walked up to the three in the front. He tapped Eddie on the shoulder, "Eddie, if there's one odor I'm familiar with--"

"Yeah, man, we smell it too."

"You see anything up there?"

"Not yet. Just more of the same."

After a few more steps they practically froze. At the end of the bridge were about three-dozen deaders staggering in their direction.

41 NOW OR NEVER

Clem was up and pacing about the cell. His movement had excited the dead, renewed their interest whether or not it ever waned. Danni was asleep. Topher was reaching for his toes. Keith was lying on his back, staring at the ceiling. Davis was watching the dead following Clem around the cell. They shifted depending on where he was in the cell. They didn't seem to understand that he would come back around. It reminded him of a certain cat his niece had, always following around a red light from a laser pointer.

"Clem. Do me a favor. Stand in that corner. Keith, please do the same. Topher you too."

"What for?"

"Just do it. I want to see what these dumb zombies do. That's it, now squeeze in, don't be shy."

"Yeah, they're following us. So? Isn't that what they've been doing?"

"It is, but look, they're not trying to get in by the gate or anything, they're following you around the room as if they had the chance of getting you. And look at the gate. They're not even blocking it anymore. Like they have no concept of it."

"You think we can get out somehow?"

"I don't know yet. There's too many to get around though, and no idea what's out of eyesight."

"Anything's better than sitting in here. How much longer can we stay in here like this?"

"Maybe one of us can give it a try? We can try to get their

attention while one of us runs out and gets around them, but I think once one of us is out there we won't be able to keep their attention. Then whoever gets out will have to lure them away so the rest of us can get out."

"I would've called you all crazy, but that seems like the best thing we can do. And Keith is right; we can't last much longer in here. I'm getting real thirsty and the thirstier I get the more I keep looking at that toilet and keep thinking that maybe, just maybe I'll be thirsty enough to drink what's in there," said Clem.

"Thanks for that thought, old timer, you just gave me one more reason to volunteer my ass for this crazy escape plan."

"Maybe we should wait. If these things thin out a bit we'll have a better chance," Davis suggested, hoping Keith would agree and sit back down.

"Wait till when? More could show up too. There's no reason to wait," Keith replied.

"Fine. We'll give it a shot, but is there some way we can take some of them down without taking the last few rounds? Anyone got a screwdriver by any chance?"

"There's nothing in here, Bruce, let's just get on with it while I still have the balls to do it."

"Fine."

They exchanged a quite moment, the hard lines in their faces softening just a touch, as they looked at each other for what they figured might just be the last time.

Davis broke away. He walked over to the cell door, reaching his hand through the bars and putting the key into the lock. The dead things grasped at his arms and hand but he was able to put the key into the lock and pull back without them getting a good hold.

"Wait till we get them good and worked up. Then, run like a motherfucking bull and tear ass out of here. Don't look back. I'll close the gate, you just keep going."

"Fuck. I think I'm gonna throw up."

"Everyone into the far corner. Get 'em worked up. Keith, hang back with us," Davis commanded.

They squished into the corner, yelling at the dead, getting them worked up. The dead smashed into each other, fighting to get closer to their would-be prey. The dead reached through the bars, grasping at air with stiff fingers. Their limbs were greying, covered in dried blood and bodily fluids. Their fingers had missing fingernails and shredded tips, broken fingers and some even had bones jutting from their forearms.

"Come and get it!" Davis yelled.

Clem had already lost his voice, but continued to yell anyway.

Keith looked at the dead. They had left a wide berth near the gate, but he couldn't tell how far back they were. He could only hope they had given him enough space to get around them.

It's now or never.

Keith ran for the door, reaching out and unlocking it in one swift movement. He flung the gate open and ran as fast and as hard as he could. The others continued to yell at the dead, in the hopes of keeping their attention, but some of them followed Keith's movements and were almost on him as he left the cell.

Davis ran for the door as a deader shambled inside. He tried to push it out, but another came up right behind it and prevented it. Then he decided to pull the first deader inside, throwing it to the floor and closing the gate before the other was in too deep. By the time he closed the door several deaders on the other side had swarmed over to it.

By the time Keith reached the wall on the far side of the room a handful of deaders had gotten in his way. Convinced he could just push past them, he ran and charged them with his head down as if he were carrying a football. He pushed past one, then another, even a third, but by the time he hit the fourth several more had fallen back from the larger group and closed off his exit.

He took out his handgun and fired once, blowing out the brains of deader number four. This made all the deaders in the room turn towards him, instantly surrounding him. He fired again, and then again, but he was out of rounds. He turned to run back to the cell but there was nowhere to go.

He tried to charge through them but couldn't. They swarmed him, pulling at his skin as he shrieked in pain. He fell to the ground, trying to crawl again when one bit his side, then his leg. Another grabbed his face, his neck. They pulled, scratching, scraping, tearing. The howls of pain filled the room, echoing in the holding cell.

They spun him around on his back despite how valiantly he fought. Their fingers tore open his shirt. They ripped out his eyes, bit out his throat and their rough, weathered fingers tore open the skin of his abdomen, exposing his fatty tissue and muscle fiber. They ripped through that just the same and began to eviscerate him, pulling out handfuls of intestines. Their teeth ripped through his intestines as if it were sausage. He screamed no more.

Davis was on his knees screaming through the bars but to no avail. The dead were all preoccupied with eating his friend.

Topher and Clem were struggling with the deader inside the cell. Its innards were spilling out all over them. They had no weapon in which to dispatch of the deader and Davis was not responding to their calls for help. Topher tried to push it to the ground, but he only managed to push it against the wall. His hands were growing slimy in gore.

It was too confined of an area to really knock it down, at least for Topher. Who was shorter than Clem and apparently no stronger. They could hear Keith screaming, and as horrible as it was they had to keep their attention on the deader in their midst. Clem tried to kick it in the knees but the deader only fell forward slightly. He did it again and Topher pushed it off balance but that only ended up with the deader falling over and taking Clem with it, spilling the rest of its innards all over him.

Danni screamed and ran over. Clem was on his back trying to push the deader away as it snapped its jaw at him. Clem was pushing its head up and Topher was pulling it off as Danni tried to pull Clem away but then it bit down on Clem's palm as his grip slipped off the deaders slimy chin.

He barely felt it, but could see the blood trickle down.

Davis finally turned around and emptied the last of his rounds into the deaders head, decorating the cell wall with brains and blood.

Danni cradled Clem as he held his bleeding hand. She cried for him as he stared at his hand, looking at the bite mark that just barely broke the skin on his palm.

"Shit," Davis said as he slumped to the ground.

"Why didn't you help them?!" Danni screamed.

Davis had no answer. He just looked at her as she lashed out at him. He could hear the sounds of the deaders slurping on Keith's remains. He was out of rounds for his firearm. He was out of ideas, and didn't know what the hell he was going to do when Clem turned into one of them.

42 SUICIDE RUN

"Do they see us?"

"Don't know, maybe they seen the fires."

"What the fuck are we going to do?"

"I have an idea."

"Which is...?"

"We're going to have to run on top of the cars till we can get passed them."

"That's your fucking idea."

"I'll go first. That should get their attention on me. When they start following me, get everyone off this bridge and get around them as fast as you can."

"Wait, that's fucking crazy."

"Ed, just do it. We can't go back. Just turn around and look. It's this or nothing."

Eddie turned around to see the smaller pack of smoldering dead shambling closer. By the time Eddie turned back around Frankie had started running toward the larger horde of deaders.

"Frankie!"

"Keep it down, Eddie," Joseph said. "He's right man, someone needs to draw them away so we can get out of here."

"It didn't have to be him."

"Man, can't you see it. He's loving this shit."

Frankie broke into a sprint. He started smacking his pry-bar on the vehicles he passed. The dead started to take notice. Once they did Frankie climbed up on top of a car and began making his way among them.

"Come and get me you dead fucks! Dinner time!"

He jumped from a car hood to the trunk of another, then into the bed of a pickup. The dead were reaching for him, gathering around him. Grunting excitedly.

"You want some of this? Come and fucking get it!"

The dead had no idea that the others were slowly moving forward as Frankie led them astray like bait on a hook.

"He's going to get himself killed," Judy said.

"That idiot will get us all killed!" Carrie screamed.

"Let's get everyone out of harm's way first. Then we'll see if there's anything we can do for him."

"It's working. They're following him."

Frankie smacked a deader's hand out of the way with his pry bar as it reached for his leg. Then he jumped to another car and ran atop a few more, getting some distance from the bulk of the horde and calling out to the others that were still a distance from him.

"Come on! COME ON! Come and get it!"

He thrust the pry bar down onto one of the deader's heads as it tried to climb onto the car. He almost lost his balance as the dead thing slumped to the ground.

Eddie and the others were staying low and moving forward, being careful not to take away any of the attention Frankie had been working hard to earn.

Frankie neared the end of the bridge. He could see the railway that ran along the coast, cutting underneath the Tappan Zee. It was too high to jump down, but he was close enough to end of the bridge where he could escape it if he were alone by simply outrunning the dead. He looked back at the group. He could just barely make out Eddie and Joseph squatted behind a car. They were moving closer, but he knew he still had to draw the deaders further away.

He jumped over to another car and then another. A deader grabbed hold of his ankle in mid stride and brought Frankie down onto the hood of a car. He lost his breath and smacked his head down hard enough to disorient but he was able to kick away the deaders face as it went in to bite his ankle. Frankie broke free and scrambled up the car. He checked himself for a bite or scratch that maybe he wasn't aware of. He found nothing. He moved to another car, and the horde of dead followed desperately.

A scream pierced the night.

Frankie turned to see what had happened but saw nothing.

Janice pulled Yussef by the arm as a deader from underneath a car grabbed at his leg, nearly pulling his sneaker off. The boy screamed again and Janice kicked the deader's arm off and pulled the boy to safety. The dead thing grabbed at her too and she fell to the ground. Jon watched in terror as he ran over and dispatched the deader just right before it could bite down on her.

The horde that Frankie tried so desperately to lead away now splintered off. He was able to keep most of them entertained enough to stick around, but several deaders shambled in the direction of the others.

"Come and get it!" Frankie yelled, hoping to draw them back, but to no avail.

Eddie and Joseph stormed forward and went on the offensive.

"Let's make this shit quick."

Scott turned to the rest of the group; "I think the only way we're getting out of here alive is if we follow Frank's lead. We can't fight them all. We need to move while they're divided and while we still have the opportunity."

"Fuck it, let's do it," Jon-Jon said, trying to psyche himself up and encourage the others.

He then ran toward Eddie and Joseph and hopped onto a small sedan, "Fuck them things guys, we're gonna run for it."

Eddie turned in disbelief as Jon-Jon jumped onto the hood of a Toyota Corolla. Following behind him was Scott, Judy, and the rest of the group.

"Holy fuck," Joseph said, "this is nuts."

Eddie then bashed one of the deaders in the face, knocking it back into the others, "Let's do it. Get up there."

Joseph cut into the line and hopped up on the sedan. Eddie swung again at the next deader, watching as Joseph helped his mother and Yussef onto the car.

"Today people, today!"

Chuck and Chung-Hee came over to Eddie and helped him take care of the first few deaders that were of immediate concern. The space was tight, but they were able to bash their heads into pulp as

Joseph helped the rest of the group up the sedan.

After seeing the rest of the group hop onto the vehicles Frankie started moving away. The deaders were no longer so concerned with him and had spread out to go after the new meat that had presented itself. Scott and Judy both took off, leaping a few vehicles ahead of the rest of the group. Jon-Jon hung around to make sure the others were getting across okay, but by doing so he ended up slowing everyone down—effectively creating a bottleneck.

As the group was held up and moving slowly across the cars the deaders reached up. One grabbed Eddie by the pant leg and was able to pull him and cause him to lose his balance. The dead thing continued to pull and Eddie fell back and was pulled down and off the car. He hit his head on the hood and was pulled to the ground.

"Eddie!"

Chuck jumped down, kicking the deaders back. Chung-Hee jumped down and smashed the deader that had pulled Eddie down and was about to rend his flesh. Chung-Hee smashed its head into the ground, knocking out teeth, and pulled Eddie up to his feet.

No one else had noticed and continued moving forward. The three of them got back on the sedan and cautiously followed behind.

43 TEETH AND GLASS

The group had become very spread apart across the tops of vehicles. Frankie had made a break for it, jumping down off a truck and fighting off a few zombies till he was off the bridge. He was still a ways off from being off the road, but at least now he had greater mobility. He could see the others making it across the cars and wasn't sure what to do next. He knew he couldn't hang around. It would only make it harder for the others to get away unscathed.

The numbers of deaders was closer to two-dozen now and the majority of them were spread out trying to get the others. Frankie still had his admirers as well and he was eager to show them a good time, but bashing their brains out would only serve as a distraction. He was shaking with adrenaline as it was, so he knew he would get nothing from it either.

He started jogging down 287, trying to look ahead, hoping to find a light in the darkness. All he could see were a row of clogged tollbooths. Looming behind that and overhead was Broadway, looking as congested as the rest of the roadway. Then he saw it—the point where he knew they could get off the bridge and toward the marina—the roof of the toll offices.

He looked back, with hope glimmering in his eyes, and could see Scott and Judy not far behind now. They had made great time across the vehicles.

"Frankie, what are we doing?" Scott shouted.

"I think we can get down over here."

"Lead the way, let's go."

"We can't just go, I'm going to wait for--"

"Just go, we'll only be getting in the way. Look how many of those fuckers are coming this way."

"Go on then, I'll stay here. Jump down and see if you can find us some wheels."

Scott jumped down off a car, shouldering a deader out of the way, then turned back to offer Judy a hand but she had already jumped down on her own and was running ahead of her husband.

"Come on," she huffed.

They ran over to Frankie who was near the guardrail overlooking the toll offices.

"It's only a few feet down. Doesn't look too bad over here."

"It's dark as shit man."

"Yeah, but I don't see any deaders and rows of abandoned cars do you?"

"No."

"Scott, how about that utility truck?"

"As good as any. Let's check it out." Scott said as he hopped up and over the guardrail.

Judy took his hand and he pulled her over, catching her as she jumped down.

Frankie turned back to the others. Joseph and Jon-Jon were in the lead, hopping from one vehicle to the other easily and cautiously. Joseph was swatting away the deaders as Jon-Jon assisted Dawn, Alexis, and two kids whose names he couldn't remember as they hopped over.

Several deaders had shambled closer to Frankie now. He was starting to settle down from his adrenaline rush, so charged over to one of the deaders and punched the pry bar right between its eyes. The dead thing grabbed his wrist but Frankie grunted and pushed the pry bar further in till the deader dropped to the gravel. He put his foot on its chest and pulled the bar out as black gunk dripped off of it. He then proceeded to hit it a few more times, but had to back up as the rest of the deaders drew closer.

"This is the worst...idea...I've ever..." Carrie couldn't finish her thought. Her chest felt tight and she couldn't get enough air in her lungs to catch her breath. Carrie hadn't done this much exercise since she was a teenager and now she was wishing she'd at least made some sort of attempt. She was once a tiny peppy cheerleader, but now she looked—and felt—more like an ox.

As she was about to hop onto the next car a deader rose up and wrapped its arms around her leg. She screamed, falling forward, and smashed her face—open mouthed—into the rear windshield of the next car. Her face was cut to shreds as the window spider-webbed. She was barely conscious. Her mouth was oozing blood and spit. Several of her teeth lay amongst the shards of glass. She almost didn't feel the deader gnawing on her calf.

Eddie ran to her, Chuck right at his side. He kicked the deader off the car and pulled Carrie out of the wreckage.

"Carrie?!"

She only mumbled. Her eyes were closed and she was making no attempt to wake up out of her stupor.

"Shit man, what do we do?"

Chuck shook his head. He didn't know what do say.

"She's as good as dead, man," Chung-Hee said, coming up from the rear.

"You're right."

"So, we're just gonna leave her?"

"I'd put her out of her misery if I could…"

The deader tried to climb up the car again, this time with a few more of its dead friends.

"No time. It sucks, Ed, but we got to go. At least she's knocked out."

Eddie's eyes fill with tears, "Not quite."

He lifted the tire iron high above his head, "Keep moving," he told them, and then bashed her in the head enough times that when the deaders dragged her off the car and to the ground she wouldn't feel a thing.

Another deader reached for Abdul but he stomped on its hand and then kicked it away. Chris still slept on his shoulders, jostling with every movement. Abdul didn't know how it was possible, but he thanked Allah all the same.

44 SKIN MASK

Danni cradled the old man in her arms. The bleeding on his hand had pretty much stopped, not that he could really tell, but he felt a new sensation in his body. His stomach felt as if he'd taken a few shots of Wild Turkey and a bad headache was percolating just behind his eyes.

"It's okay, Danielle, I'll be with Lorraine again. We'll keep an eye on you."

"I know you will. You'll both be happy again—it just sucks that this had to happen in here…now…you know? It's just not fair."

"Yeah, I know. I guess I figured I'd just die in a hospital bed. Warm sun coming through the window. A get well soon balloon tied to the foot of the bed. All the typical stuff."

"Does it hurt?"

"My hand? No."

"Not your hand, you know what I mean."

"Not much."

Davis was starting to feel guilty about the old man's bite. His duty was to protect people. All he ever wanted to do was to protect people who couldn't protect themselves. And for the most part he was happy with what he'd been able to do. But when he momentarily gave into despair and ignored their pleading for help he might as well have killed him himself.

He looked over at them out of the corner of his eye. He wanted to apologize, to offer some words of comfort, but he knew they would be meaningless. They were going to die in here and that was that. He resigned himself to that fate and closed his eyes, hoping he'd wake up dead.

Topher stared at the dead body in the cell. Whoever the man was in his former life kept himself in good shape. His neck was like a tree and his biceps were bigger than Topher's head.

He stared at the gore and then to the dead. A crazy thought popped into his head and wondered if it was just plain crazy, or crazy to where it might actually work. He crawled over to the deader hesitantly. Nervous, he was afraid it would jump up and scare the shit out of him.

It didn't. He looked over his arm, making sure he had no cuts or scrapes that he wasn't aware of. Then he stuck his hand into the exposed cavity of the deader's head and pulled out a handful of brain and goo that instantaneously made him want to vomit. He then began to smear it all over his arm. He reached in for more of the viscous contents and did the same—lather, repeat.

"Ohmygod, what the fuck are you doing? Are you insane?"

Davis opened his eyes.

"I have an idea."

"Have you lost your fucking mind?"

"Possibly, but I have to give it a try."

"Give what a try? Are you going to eat that shit?"

"What? No! I'm going to see if this can act like a camouflage."

"Please tell me you have no intention of making a skin mask next?" Davis asked.

"A what?"

"Skin mask. Mask made out of skin. Like Ed Gein…serial killer."

"That's not a bad idea. But first just a trial test…if you will."

Topher, content with the amount of gore covering his arm and hand walked over to the cell bars. He waived his hand around at the deaders seeing if they would grab it. Unsure if they were going after him or his hand he went closer. He stuck out both arms, almost mimicking the way they walk and from the looks of it, they preferred the cleaner arm. He moved closer, close enough to where they could grab him. They ignored the limb covered in human remains and tried to get his other arm.

"Ha! I think it could work."

"You think covering yourself in bloody remains will get us out of here?"

"Well, I don't think there's enough to go around, but maybe. I don't know if I want to cover my entire body in this shit. Especially my face, I can't see a way around that without getting into my eyes and mouth, and then I'm sure that'll get me turned into a zombie. But if you have any other ideas, please."

"I got nothing, but if I were you, I'd clean that shit off."

"Of course."

Topher looked around the room. There was only the toilet.

"Detainees don't need a sink?"

"Not in here they don't. It's just a holding cell for fuck's sake."

Giving a deep sigh he walked over to and knelt by the toilet. He reached his hands in and began to wash off the gore, flushing it down and trying to not to vomit. He wasn't sure what was worse. Sticking his hand in a dead man's head, or a toilet.

"I hope he doesn't try wearing my innards after I go," Clem joked.

Danni smiled at first and then the smile turned into a hard frown, "I'm gonna miss you."

"I'll miss you too, but we'll see each other again I'm sure. You think they have reruns of Cheers in heaven?"

"In heaven, I would think they'd have new episodes."

"Now yer talkin'."

45 GOODBYE, NEW JERSEY

More and more people from the group were able to get to Frankie at the edge of the road. Frankie was directing them down toward the toll offices. He wanted to wait till Eddie was with him, but he wasn't sure how much longer he'd be able to stick around. The deaders were continuing to make their way over to him, and no matter how much adrenaline was pumping through his veins he was exhausted. His blows were growing weaker and his arms burned as if he'd been lifting weights all day.

Moments later the rest of the group was visible. Eddie, Chuck, and Chung-Hee hopped from one vehicle to the other. Frankie waived his hands in the air, jumping and yelling, "Let's go motherfuckers!"

Eddie looked up, as he jumped down from the last car before running towards Frankie and his deader admirers. He ran at him, clobbering a deader in the back of the head and knocking it forward with his tire iron as Chung-Hee ran atop of it, making sure it stayed down.

"This way. Over the side," Frankie yelled as he straddled over the guardrail and jumped the few feet down.

Chuck didn't even slow down to look before he leapt. He ran right up to the guardrail, planting his foot and then jumping into the air over the side.

Chung-Hee followed behind, though he and Eddie both paused before jumping off the side. Seeing it was clear and not that far down they hopped over and jumped down. Joining the others as they ran toward the toll offices.

***

Scott and Judy had found a maintenance truck parked out front. It could fit three people inside across the bench seat, and if everyone else jumped into the bed of the truck they might be able to fit. There were no keys inside the vehicle, so they went inside the building. Jon-Jon joined them and as soon as Joseph made it down from the bridge he did too. Everyone else waited outside anxiously.

Scott opened the door slowly and quietly, trying to listen for any noise inside the building. On the outside it was a small building with a lot of windows, but inside it was dark and seemed cavernous.

They crept forward. Now trying to move fast, but without making much noise.

"Look for any keys," Scott whispered.

Judy nodded, sweeping her head around the room, hoping they would just jump out at her.

"I'll check these desks," Jon said, skirting past them and to the side.

It looked like a receptionists desk. There was a charging station with several walkie-talkies and a telephone. An old bulky computer monitor took up most of the desk and a coffee cup full of pens sat next to it. No keys. He rummaged through the drawers—No keys.

Scott opened another door—this one leading to an office. The manager's he figured by the looks of it. He doubted he'd find the key in there but he had to look. Judy stood by him, checking a row of cabinets as he checked out the desk.

Joseph looked around. He didn't want to go about looking for the keys blindly. He thought about it, as if he were looking for his own keys, which he would always lose around the house. He always left them in his pockets—pants pockets, jackets, coats, things like that. If he just came in from driving the truck what would he do? Take off his coat. Get changed. Go home.

He spun around and then he saw it—a coat rack. Come on, please be in here. He rushed over to it. There were four jackets. A woman's pea coat, a navy blue trench coat, a Carhartt, and a track jacket. He grabbed the Carhartt and rummaged through the pockets; a pack of bubblegum, a pack of cigarettes and a lighter, a pen, and a set of keys.

"Yo!" He yelled, overly excited. " I found a set of keys," he said much quieter.

"Go see if they work," Jon-Jon said, still looking around in case they weren't the right ones.

Joseph grabbed the coats and ran outside. He tossed the coats to the group, "If you're cold, grab one. Check the pockets too."

He hopped into the truck, trying to fit each key into the hole. Eventually one of them slid right in. He turned the ignition and the truck roared to life. He slapped the steering wheel and as he was about to honk the horn, Scott, Judy, and Jon-Jon came running out of the building.

"Fuck yea!" Jon-Jon shouted.

"Everyone in," Judy yelled.

Scott and Judy ran to the front seat.

Jon-Jon ran to Dawn, "Come on, let's get in the back."

***

Joseph spun the truck around, being mindful of the passengers in the back, and pulled around as his brother and the others came down from the bridge.

"About time, get the fuck in."

They climbed in and Joseph started driving away.

Jon tapped on the window to the back of the cab and Scott opened it up. "We need to follow the train tracks up the Hudson to get to the marina. Go towards the water and make a right."

Scott gave him a thumbs-up and relayed the message to Joseph.

"Guys," Jon said, "it's going to get real bumpy once we get to them tracks so we all need to hold on tight."

46 THAT SAD SMILE

Joseph slowed the truck down as it bounced on the rocky terrain. The moonlight on the water lit the area well and Joseph was able to see the train tracks without a problem. The tracks ran underneath the bridge and they reminded him of all the times he'd gone drinking down by the tracks back home—when he had a home.

He then drove the truck along the tracks following them toward the marina Jon had spoke about. Which couldn't have been too far away considering he could see the sails of some of the boats in the water, but he guessed those could just be adrift.

"I like the idea of being on a boat."

"Me too, I always wanted one."

"Well, now you can get one okay?"

"Better late than never."

"Did you have a boat Joe?"

"Me, no…my, uh, my dad used to have one when we were kids. I don't remember what happened with it exactly, but he got rid of it. I think it was too expensive and he wasn't using it much. He wanted to get another one when he retired."

"Oh, I'm sorry Joe…"

"It's okay. Maybe he's got that boat now."

"I bet he does."

"He's probably got himself a Mojito and a line in the water."

"Yeah, man, he'd love that. Just kicking back…finally."

After a quite moment, one of reflection for Joseph, and one of trepidation for Scott and Judy, Joseph asked, "So how long do you think it'll take us to get out of here once we're on the water?"

"Hours. The longest part will probably be getting out of the Hudson, but once we get into the open waters we can just follow the coast up and be near Maine in a few hours."

"Cool. I just want to sleep for a few days."

"That sounds good."

"I want a nice hot bath first, and then to sleep."

Janice held her hand around her ankle as she sat cross-legged in the bed with Yussef in her lap. She didn't think the scratch would've been enough to turn her into a deader, but she could feel something wrong inside her. She stared at her son and smiled, trying not to cry.

Eddie smiled back, thinking she was just happy to get off the bridge, but he knew that smile. He knew that wasn't a happy smile. There was something else in it—sadness. It reminded him of the day his grandmother died. She smiled at him that day. She was happy to see him, but she had the bad news to deliver. It was that same smile.

"What's wrong?"

She didn't want to say anything. Not around the others. "You're all grown up, Edward."

Her eyes were wet and her lips were dry.

"Mom…"

"I remember when you and your brother were small. The two of you were joined at the hip, always playing with your toy guns, and all those little figures. You'd leave them all over the place. I used to hate stepping on them. They hurt like hell, and it must've took ten years for you two to ever pick them up on your own. Probably seems like a lifetime ago to you doesn't it. Well, it seems like yesterday to me. It all went by so fast. Too fast, sweetheart."

"We're fine mom, everything is going to be okay, you'll see."

"I know. You remember the boat your father used to have?"

"Of course."

"He used to love the smell of the water. We used to be able to sit out there all day. I would read, and you three would do your fishing. You probably don't remember, but your father and I started talking about having other children back then. It took a long time to happen, but that's kind of where…"

Eddie moved over to his mother and held her as she broke down into tears, "It's gonna be okay, Mom, it's gonna be…okay."

Janice put her hand on her son's face and looked up at him, "You keep your brother safe. Keep him close, just like you used to be. You hear me?"

"I will."

"It'll just be the two of you soon."

"What are you talking about?"

"I'm dying, sweetheart. I can feel it."

"Wh—how?"

"On the bridge. When that thing tried to get me and the boy."

Eddie tried to hold it all in. He didn't want to accept what he was hearing, "No. No, fuck no. You weren't bit."

"It scratched my ankle, I didn't even know it right away. Then I started to feel it. It kinda feels like being hungry, but I'm not."

"Does it hurt?"

"No baby."

"Are you scared?"

"Not really. I'll get to be with our family again. Your daddy's probably waiting for me. The kid's are probably driving him nuts, especially if there's no beer in heaven."

"There better be, or he'll be pretty pissed off."

"If I survive the boat trip, son, I want you to do something for me."

"Anything."

"I want a funeral. I want you to cremate me and I won't really care how. Scatter me somewhere nice if you can. Just don't leave me walking around or mangled up somewhere."

Eddie simply nodded and held her tight.

Yussef had moved off of Janice's lap and nuzzled up to Alexis. They, along with everyone else in the back of the truck, watched as Janice continued to cry into her son's shirt. It should've been an intimate moment, but there was no privacy to give. Even those who looked away still heard every word.

Joseph could see the marina. There were plenty of boats docked, rocking gently on the silvery black water.

"We're so fucking close, babe."

Judy kissed him hard and bounced with excitement, ready to open the door and run out to any one of the boats out there.

47 IT'S ALWAYS CROWDED

Walter, Jeff, and Barbara drove around town, weaving through the familiar streets. Deaders staggered about like they were tumbleweeds blowing in the wind. The sound of the truck alerted them, and as they found where the noise came from, Walter drove on past.

They drove past a car with bloodied handprints and streaks all along the windows and doors, but no one was inside. They past homes boarded up but appearing bare of life. Storefronts were adorned with broken windows and the streets were littered with signs of the living dead.

"Maybe there isn't anyone left," Barbara suggested.

"It does look pretty dead out there, pardon the phrase," her father replied.

"Let's just head back toward home," Jeff said, "we can get back to scavenging for supplies."

"I don't want to just give up like that," Walter said, "there just has to be a few people left. They're probably just too scared to go outside."

"Well, it's your gas, I guess," Jeff said, eyeing the gauge which Walter never let go further than halfway before refilling.

***

"I ain't feelin' so hot anymore," said Clem, sounding like a bullfrog.

"You've got a heck of a fever, and your sweating."

"I don't know how much longer I got. Starting to feel like I got the flu or something."

Danni was about to break down again, but she held strong. Not for herself, but for Clem. He'd been a rock throughout everything. He needed her to keep her shit together now and she was determined to do so.

"What can I do?"

"Nothing you can do kiddo, except to get the hell out of here."

"Do you feel like you're turning into one?"

"Not yet, but I can't imagine it's far behind. Topher...come here, will ya?"

"Whattya need, Clem?"

"Can you help me get covered in that shit?"

"What? Clem no."

"Danni, I got to get you out of here. I'm dying. I can feel it tearing me up inside. Way I see it is I'm so close to death those things won't want to bother with me. If Topher can cover me from head to toe in that filth than maybe I can get you out of here. Give my death a little more purpose. Hell, maybe I can see daylight one last time."

"And what if it doesn't work. You shouldn't have to go out in pain like that. Them eatin..."

"Shhh. I want to do this, I don't want to die in here, okay?"

"O-okay." She said, hugging him so tightly he began to cough. She then kissed him on the forehead and turned to Topher.

"You ready?"

"No, but let's get on with it."

"Clem...I'm...I'm sorry..."

"Don't sweat it Sheriff. You just make sure she gets out of here and we'll call it even. If that thing didn't bite me, we might all have died in here anyway."

Topher knelt by the twitching corpse in the middle of the cell. Clem, ushered over by Danni, stood just behind him.

"You care if I stand? Not sure if I take a knee that I'll be able to get back up."

"That's fine, want to hold out your hands?"

Clem stood there with his hands cupped together as Topher dug into the dead man's body. He piled clumps of grey matter and goo into Clem's hands and Clem started to rub it onto his body. Danni backed away and started dry heaving. Had she eaten anything it would've certainly come up.

The dead man's head was pretty much cleaned out but Topher scooped out what he could and dropped it into Clem's hands. The man's stomach was ripped to shreds and most of his guts were already on the ground, but Topher managed to pull out fatty tissue and clumps of coagulated blood that clung to the inside of his body.

His mind was somewhere else but every once and a while it came back and wondered just where and what his hands were doing. It felt like he was watching himself do this as opposed to doing it.

Topher wrapped his hand around what he guessed was the man's lower intestines and began to pull it out of the widening whole in the large man's stomach. It smelled terribly and once he saw his hands pulling out more than a foot of intestine he vomited all over the corpse. He couldn't believe how many feet of intestine were still inside as he pulled it out, still vomiting as he did so.

Danni was retching again in the corner and now Clem was starting to heave as well. Davis just sat and watched in some disconnected state of reality.

Clem took the rope of intestine from Topher and it almost slid out of his hands. He pulled it up and draped it over his shoulder. Topher ripped into it with his fingers, and Clem draped it around his neck like a scarf. Topher pulled out more and more and Clem continued to drape it atop himself.

By the time they had Clem covered in gore everyone had vomited several times over. The floor was one giant puddle of blood and vomit and Clem stood like some sort of monster covered in ropes of intestine, blood, and chunks of random gore. Aside from the whites of his eyes there wasn't a clean spot on him.

He stood near the door of the cell, his fever burning hot. He felt as if he wanted to collapse but as the dead paid him no attention he knew that he could not. He wasn't entirely sure if it was that Topher's idea solely had worked or if it was the combination of that and Clem being so near death.

The rest of them crowded into the corner yelling at the dead. The dead tried again to grasp their prey. Clem turned the key and slowly opened the door. Not a one turned to look. He stepped out, his legs burning with each movement. He closed the door, and looked back inside once at Danni and only Danni. She was crying, and so was Clem now. He turned back and began to walk around them. In a few steps she lost sight of him.

He walked slowly and staggered on his own.

I'm coming home, Lorraine.

He was behind the dead now, and going around them. They didn't seem to care.

Once out of sight he began singing in a raspy terrible voice. He sounded like Tom Waits with bronchitis.

Heartbreak Hotel was one of the few songs he could remember all of the words to. Not that he was a big fan of The King, but just because it was one of those songs that got stuck in his head and never left, so he went with it and began belting out the verses. He smashed things and kicked things and threw the intestines off his body, trying to make as much noise as possible so that the dead would follow him on out as if he were the Pied Piper.

He tiredly pushed aside what was left of the barricade by the front doors and stepped outside. He stared at the sun, singing as loud as he could. He could hear the dead shambling behind him now. They were starting to follow the noise.

"...And although it's always crowded, You still can find some room, Where broken hearted lovers, Do cry away their gloom..."

"He did it, they're leaving, and following him out."

"Don't get too excited, just hold on and keep quiet. Keep listening, and when I tell you, run like hell."

***

Barbara had taken a turn behind the wheel, hoping she'd have better luck coming across someone than her father was having. She drove toward the outskirts of town, near the VFW hall. She slowed the truck down to a crawl, just long enough to survey the dead twitching bodies scattered around the grounds. Walter peered out the window, taking note of the police cruiser that looked as if it had been in a war, covered in blood, dirt, and dents.

He shook his head and Barbara drove on.

48 THE PROTEAN

Several deaders were shambling around the front of the marina. They lurched with weary limbs. Joseph and Frankie took the lead, running out to greet the deaders while they were still spread apart. Chuck followed behind.

Frankie smashed one across the face, knocking its jaw nearly off, spinning it off balance and then kicking it to the ground. He swept out the knees of another and as he was about to go for a third, Chuck swung into action and knocked the dead thing down first. Joseph was bashing a deaders head into pulp and Frankie and Chuck were doing the same to the ones they had knocked down, turning them into a twitching mass of black blood and putrefying remains.

Scott, Judy, and Jon led the group through the carnage, while the others finished off the remaining deaders. The marina office itself was a small building that sat right near the water. To the left of them was a ramp that led to the side of the building and most likely to the dock behind it. Scott jogged over and waived everyone on.

"This way. The coast is clear."

Frankie caught up to the lead, Joseph not far behind him. Joseph looked back to see where his mother and brother were. He noticed the two of them walking side by side and that something seemed off. His brother was usually in the midst of the action, taking charge. It seemed like he didn't care what was happening.

"Joe, there's a few over here."

He turned and ran over to Frankie. Behind the building was an outside patio. Many of the tables had been overturned and thrown about. Some where bloodied but most were not.

"Chuck…take point and find us a boat," Frankie yelled.

Chuck then ran ahead to the dock, eyeing the offerings for one that would be able to fit everyone—or as many of them as possible.

"I'll come with you," Jon-Jon called out.

The night wind coming off of the water was cool and salty, but there was the hint of something else…something dead.

"I smell it too," Jon said, "Let's hurry the fuck up."

"Not going to be that easy. The dock isn't exactly full, and we got a few people here. Most of what I'm seeing can't carry all of us."

"Can you walk us through how to drive one?"

"Honestly. It's a lot harder than I made it sound earlier, but I'm sure we can find something. It's not like we need to adhere to the SOLAS convention, we can just cram into a smaller vessel. We're used to sitting on top of each other."

"That we are. What the hell's a SOLAS?"

"It's just about passenger safety."

"Yeah, well, we can forget about that."

Chuck paused, stopping at the start of a new row, "Right there," he pointed.

"You ever drive something like that?"

"I basically lived on something like that. Want to go check it for deaders?"

"Not really, but let's do it."

They jogged ahead as the group followed cautiously behind.

Joseph had finished dispatching of the deaders in the area and joined his mother and brother who were lingering near the back of the group.

"Hey, what's a matter with you two?"

"Sorry, sweetheart. I told your brother while you were driving…"

Joseph looked back and forth from his mother to Eddie. Looking for a clue and seeing nothing but bad news in their faces.

"…I'm dying."

"No…"

"Sorry baby. I…I got scratched on the bridge. Didn't think it was anything, but I can feel it inside me." She put her hand to his face as he began to tear up.

Eddie put his arm around his shoulder.

"I'm sorry Mom, I should've been there to make sure nothing happened to you. We should've protected you."

"It's not your fault. I want this. I want this to be over."

"You want to die?"

"No, but I do want to be with your father, and with the little ones. They still need me. You two are all grown up. Look at you both. Two big strong men."

"No, mamma…"

"Come on honey, looks like they found a boat."

"What are we gonna do Mom?"

"I told your brother what to do if I make it off the boat."

"I love you."

"I love you too, son. I love you both so much. I'm proud of you both. You both turned into two good men. I know I wasn't always perfect, but I know I raised you both right."

"It isn't fair."

"No it's not. Nothing's fair. Life isn't fair. Now stop crying and get us out of here. I don't have much time. I'm going to fight this as much as I can so we can get off that boat together. I don't want to die on the water."

Janice held both of her sons by their faces, wiping away their tears with her thumbs. "Your father would've been so proud of you both. He never said it enough—he wasn't much for the mushy stuff—but he loved you kids."

Chuck and Jon climbed onto the boat. It was a big vessel—a charter yacht—and wasn't more than a few years old. The Protean was elegantly scripted across the back of the boat.

"It's beautiful," Chuck said.

"You can drive it?"

"I can't drive it—a Captain pilots a boat."

"Ok, Chuck, can you pilot it?"

"Of course I can, but let's make sure there aren't any surprises in the cabin."

"Lead the way, Captain."

49 CAPTAIN CHUCK

Chuck and Jon came back out of the cabin as the others waited close by on the dock, huddled together. Jon waived them on board, saying "All clear."

"What about the keys?"

"We'll have to check inside the marina."

"Any volunteers?"

The usual suspects all started for the marina. Scott began helping everyone else on board.

"Ed, there's no guarantee the keys are in there. The owner might not keep them here."

"Well, then what the fuck are we supposed to do?"

"I don't know. I thought it made sense to find the boat first and then look for the keys. We have the slip number. If we just ran in and grabbed all the keys I think it'd be more chaotic to find the boat after that."

"You're probably right. But maybe we should've scouted for a back up boat?"

"Whatever guys," Frankie said. "It doesn't matter, we'd have to do this either way, right?"

That was enough to keep them quiet while they reached the patio doors of the marina. Frankie pulled the door handle and was relieved to find it opened. They stepped inside and no sooner did a pair of bloodied yuppies wearing bloodied boat shoes and Dockers come staggering out at them. Frankie was quick to attack and so was Joseph. They both took down their dead attackers and mashed their faces into the floor.

"Holy shit, does it stink in here."

Chuck made his way to the counter and rifled through the key compartments.

"There's got to be another one in here. Two of 'em can't smell this bad."

"Who gives a shit? Are the keys in there or what Chuck?"

"Yes they are. I'm going to grab a few more in the same row just in case."

A door burst open in the marina. In the darkness though, no one could see from where. Joseph ran for the door and called the others to follow. Chuck pocketed a bunch of keys and they jangled as he ran over. Then a deader clutched his arm out of the darkness and Chuck howled in fear. Frankie pulled the dead thing by its greasy hair as it was about to bite down and pulled it back, throwing it against the wall. As Chuck ran for the door Frankie bashed its head against the wall so hard it cracked the sheetrock. He let go of the dead thing and followed the others out the door, wiping the greasy film off his hands and onto his pants.

Several other deaders had begun to approach the rear of the marina, seemingly emerging out of the darkness. Eddie and the others didn't bother with them and ran toward the boat.

Once on board Chuck was able to start the engine. Eddie struggled with unknotting the rope from the boat slip until he remembered he had a knife in his pocket. He dug it out and began cutting the rope but it was too big and proving to be just as difficult. Chuck jumped down and helped him out.

"Thanks man," that was one hell of a knot."

"Well, I'm sure the owner didn't want it drifting away on him."

"Probably not."

"Should we give these guys a lift?" Chuck joked, pointing at the approaching deaders.

Eddied forced a laugh and then followed him onto the boat.

Frankie stood on the deck, looking down into the water. It was dark, and the waters were still, but he could see something just below the surface. At first he wasn't sure if it was the moonlight reflecting on the water, but after a few moments he was able to start making out forms. He looked on both sides and off the back and finally he accepted what his eyes were trying to tell him—deaders were under the water grasping at the bottom of the boat. Disgusted and disturbed he had to make sure he wasn't going crazy and he called Eddie over.

"Ed, come here a second will ya?"

"What's up man?"

"Look in the water."

"What am I looking for?"

"Keep looking."

"Oh…"

"You see 'em?"

"Yeah, yeah I see 'em. That's pretty fucked man."

"Ok, I just wanted to make sure I wasn't seeing shit."

"Everyone, get inside the cabin and make yourselves comfortable. Captain Chuck is going to get us the hell out of here."

Most of the group had already collapsed in the cabin upon boarding the boat earlier, but those that had hung around now started to make their way down into the luxurious belly of the boat.

Eddie, Joseph, Janice, Frankie, and Scott hung around up top with Chuck.

"You know where you're going?"

"Basically. Might be one hell of a sightseeing tour. We're going to have to follow the Hudson out into the Atlantic and head up the coast. Going to be weird seeing New York in darkness."

"Well I think I'll keep you company."

"Me too. Wish I had a cigar," Frankie said, scratching at his growing beard.

"I'm sure whoever had this boat has some stogies on board. In fact, there are probably all kinds of goodies down there. Actually, if any of you go down there, I could use some water or something."

"I'll go check it out," Scott offered. "If I find any drinks I'll bring a few up too."

"You the man."

Chuck piloted the boat slowly out of the dock and into the Hudson, slowly increasing speed and eventually hitting a nice cruising speed.

Scott came back up with a handful of cigars, bottles of water, and a bottle of Johnnie Walker Gold Label under his arm. Judy followed behind him with a few glasses.

"There we go," Chuck smiled. "I knew there'd be a few amenities down there."

"There's more than a few. Whoever owned this thing was a party animal. All top shelf shit too. There's two showers down there. Soap! Toothpaste, toilet paper, man we got everything."

"Don't get too attached. Hopefully we'll be off this boat before we can fully enjoy it."

"Till then I'll be dutifully dulling my senses."

50 FAREWELL

Clem stood in the middle of the street watching the dead shamble out the front doors. Their ghastly rasping made his stomach churn. The thought of becoming one of them was maddening. He felt like he was burning alive, like the sun itself was drawing closer to him. They moved closer but Clem was slow to respond, too swept away in his own aches and pains to be able to move out of the way. Though he was dying, the dead didn't seem to care so much anymore. Why they didn't bother when he escaped the cell was beyond him now. Maybe they didn't like his singing. Whatever the reason they decided they wanted what little life he had left bled out into their mouths.

Clem didn't even feel the first few rips into his flesh. It wasn't until he was on his back underweight of the horde of deaders that he knew what was happening. Only then did he begin to scream. Their dead jaws rended the flesh from his bones. Blood poured from the holes in his skin, filling in like sand on the beach after the surf comes rushing back.

"Oh God, is that Clem? Is that Clem screaming?"

"Easy, Danni, he was dying anyway. At least it will be over for him soon."

"How can you say that? That's a horrible way to die…them things eating you…"

Danni bolted out of the cell.

"Danni, no! Don't just go running out there like that. You'll get us all killed."

Davis and Topher followed her out of the cell but she was already bursting through the doors leading outside.

"No!"

She didn't listen as she ran outside. Some of the dead that had not descended upon Clem turned toward Danni as she screamed at the horror that was her friend.

Danni pushed past the first few deaders that moved for her and headed into the street towards open ground.

Davis and Topher came through the door more slowly, but upon seeing how close the deaders were they ran towards Danni. One of the deaders lurched for Topher and landed a solid grasp on his shirt, jerking him back and pulling him close enough to bite him. Topher turned to defend himself but was bit on the forearm for his troubles. He stared in disbelief as the dead thing ripped a thin patch of skin from his arm.

He pulled away and ran towards the others.

"I've been bit...I...I..."

"I saw. I'm sorry."

"Me too, man. What do you want to do?"

"Can I come with you guys?"

"Sure."

"Where are we going anyway?"

"Well, I'm going home. Then I'm coming right back here and putting everyone of these motherfuckers down."

"Someone's coming."

"Wha...Walter Caulfield. God damn."

"Come on, get to my truck. Looks like these fuckers are still hungry."

Once in Davis's truck they drove off and down the road to the approaching pick up being driven by Barbara Caulfield.

"Dad, isn't that the Sheriff?"

"Sure is. Pull up alongside them."

"Look at all those zombies," Jeff noted.

"Gotta be about two dozen of them."

"Walter. Man, am I glad to see you."

"Likewise, Sheriff. We were taking a drive to see if we could find anyone else left in town. And low and behold…"

"Tell me you would've come into the station?"

"Sure," Walter nodded, "especially if your truck was out front."

"Goddamnit, if we just sat back we'd all have made it out alive," Davis mumbled.

"What's that?"

"Just a bit of fatal irony is all. We were stuck in one of the cells—surrounded by those guys coming up behind us. Two of us didn't make it--"

"Make that three," Topher added, waiving three fingers in the air as if calling over a bartender.

"Three of us didn't make it."

"That's a shame. I wish we came here sooner, Bruce. I really do. Where are you headed to now?"

"I was gonna head home. Got a bit of an arsenal. Was going to come back and re-secure the station."

"Want a few extra hands?"

"You betcha. Follow me back to my house?"

Davis sped away, relieved to be out in the world again. Danni sat with her head against the window in a state bordering on shock. Topher sat in the back holding his wound, trying his best to think of the good times, but could only picture Clem dead on the ground and think of his future, wondering if he would share the same fate.

"Sheriff?"

"Yeah?"

"Can you put me down when I turn?"

"If that's what you want."

"Wouldn't you?"

"Not so sure. What if life on the other side isn't so bad?"

"And what if it's hell on earth?" Topher said, pondering it as the words slid out of his mouth.

"Point taken. Whatever road you want to go down, Topher, you got it."

51 LIVING DEAD

In the cabin all the children with exception to Christopher had fallen asleep. They lay huddled together on the large luxurious bed that still smelled of fresh linen. A smell many of them had forgotten till now.

Alexis rummaged through the cabinets, sorting through the clothes. She set a few pieces aside for herself and moved along as Dawn did the same. Abdul took the opportunity to shower in one of the two bathrooms and after realizing there were indeed two bathrooms—and two showers—Alexis jumped at the chance to use the other one.

"My hair is so disgusting I want to cut it off. It'll take hours to wash out all the grease."

"Well don't use all the shampoo. I'm going next."

"I'll try to save you some hot water."

Then looking around, Alexis realized that Carrie wasn't among them.

"Dawn? Did you see Carrie?"

"I don't think she made it sweetheart."

"Oh." She had grown to hate the woman. Though she didn't want her dead, part of her was relieved that she was no longer with them. "Well if you find any makeup, let me know."

"I didn't even think about that. I hope there's a pack of slims somewhere in this heap."

Alexis turned on the water. Just hearing the spray of the shower was soothing to her. As the steam started to fill the room and fog the mirror she put her leg in to feel the temperature and in seconds she stepped in. It was comforting, invigorating, and from the look of the murky water pooling at her feet, cleansing. There was a small bar of soap. The smell of it filled her nose and she realized how often she'd taken that scent for granted all her life.

She dried off in front of the mirror. With the dirt and grime washed away she almost looked like herself. Her skin felt soft and fresh and she could no longer detect her own odor. She brushed her teeth, combed her hair, and put on someone else's deodorant. She put on the new clothes she found, and despite them being a little loose and a little long they fit her good enough.

Topside, Chuck had maintained a good cruising speed. The Tappan Zee Bridge was now fading in the distance, but ahead in the dark waters of the Hudson floated any number of dangers. The Hudson grew narrow and presented a frightening view of both New York and New Jersey. Both coasts lit only by the moonlight. Boats sat adrift in the water with no signs of life. Then a boat, not far from a small dock near the coast, had a deader rise up and walk toward them, walking right off the boat and disappearing under the water with a small splash that was barely heard.

"Did you see that?"

"Yeah. Kinda funny."

"Funny, but kind of sad, don't you think? Those deaders are dumber than dirt. It just walked right off the boat. And these things are fucking destroying us."

"That just makes it even funnier."

"Come on, Frankie. How is that funnier?"

"Just is man. The whole thing is just a fucking joke."

"Everything's a joke."

"Then how come you aren't laughing?"

"I was close, that deader made me smile. Almost made me laugh. And that's a good thing, man. I didn't think I had any in me."

"Any what?"

"Laughter, hope, whatever. I thought it was all gone. Do you know why I followed you over that bridge?"

Eddie paused. Uncertain of how a single comment erupted into this.

"I followed you over because I figured we'd all end up dead. And it didn't mater anymore because I didn't feel like I was alive. It's almost like I'm one of the living dead. What's the point of going on when all we are is gone?"

Janice began to cry, "Oh, Francis, I felt the same way. I've wanted to die for too long now, and right before the bridge I wanted to live again. Something welled up inside of me just before—a little light, a little hope, I guess. I didn't want to leave you boys, I couldn't, but I didn't want to live either. Francis, boys, you can make it in this world. I can see it in you. There's a fire."

"I thought I lost it."

"Did anyone else go along just to die?"

"Fuck no," said Chuck.

Scott shook his head, holding Judy's hand as she said, "No way. We went along because we thought we could do it. Maybe not alone, but together I thought we could. Not to be a part of some suicide run."

"What about you, Joe?"

"I want to live. I want my family back, but I don't want to die. We're all going to go one day anyway, so what's the rush? I want to get back at these deaders. I want to survive them. For me, for you, for everyone they've take from us. I...I want...revenge."

"Don't live on hate, son. Please."

"I promise you I won't live on it forever."

"We lived on love a long time, Mom, because of you. You and Dad. But maybe hate's what we need right now. Maybe that's the only way we can live in this world. We've been running on fear and anger this whole time. I got some hate to give."

"Maybe you guys shouldn't be drinking then?"

"Chuck, just get us the fuck out of here, okay?"

"I'm sorry, but you guys are getting all worked up, and the last thing I need on my boat is a bunch of angry drunks."

"Nobody's drunk yet."

"Speak for yourself," Judy said, tipping back her glass.

52 A DEAD CITY BY THE SEA

The statue of liberty stood tall against the cool darkness. As Scott stared out at it he could imagine a tear rolling down her face and her feet bathed in blood. Just as dark, but not nearly as tall was Ellis Island. Lower Manhattan was nothing but shadows. Battery Park looked as quite as a graveyard. The Staten Island ferries were nowhere to be seen, and there were no passengers waiting to board.

Governor's Island seemed to have some sort of fires burning, and there was no shortage of boats docked around it.

"What's that place?" Chuck asked.

"Governor's Island."

"What is it though?"

"It was a military base for the longest time—army and coast guard I think—then they started turning it into a national park."

"Man, that would be a great place to hold up."

"Yeah, but look. Fires or lights…something. I think there are probably a few survivors over there already. Probably even military."

"Even better."

"I don't think so, Chuck. Whoever's over there is probably looking to protect their claim. We're better off sticking to our plan. Less people up north, and less problems."

"Surely others have gone north as well."

"No doubt. Want to put it up to a vote?"

"Guys? Anyone wanna weigh in?"

"Let's keep going," Eddie said.

"Can't hurt to check it out."

"North."

"Ditto."

"Doesn't matter."

"Want to bring the matter downstairs?"

"Nah, fuck it. You're right. Let's stick to the plan. Get as far away as we can."

"Anyone disagree?"

"No, but it can't hurt to take us a little closer could it?"

"Not at all," Chuck said, course correcting to bring the boat closer to the island.

"It's pretty fucked up seeing the city like this. I wonder if TC looked the same way, ya know, before it was blown to shit."

"I think everywhere looks like this. Maybe it's just making an impact because the city was always alive with lights, and now they're all gone. Just hits a little harder I guess."

"You might be right."

"Hey Scott, there's a shower downstairs, right?"

"Sure is."

"You know if there's a line?"

"Probably."

"I wanna get this fucking blood off of me."

"I bet. I'm just too exhausted to get up. My legs are jelly."

"Weren't you into hiking and shit?"

"Hiking, walking, biking. All that. But it's different when you're not eating right. Or drinking right."

"This is the best I've ever eaten. I don't know what you're talking about."

"I think the homeless eat better than we do. Or at least did."

"Hey, guys, take a look. I don't want to go in any closer."

They all stood up and looked over at Governor's Island. There were a few fires burning in the distance, but none close enough to determine their cause.

"Could be bonfires."

"Maybe they're burning the dead—cleaning up the island."

"Could be anything."

"Do you see anyone?"

"Over there, by the water."

"Where—never mind—those look like deaders coming out of the water."

"Fuck, they are."

"No. Not those. Look, walking toward the deaders."

Then automatic rifle fire filled the air and small bursts of muzzle flashes lit the night sky.

"Yup. Someone's on the island. And they got firepower."

"If that's the army, why the fuck aren't they out helping survivors?"

"Want to go ask them?"

"Fuck no."

"So we gonna keep going."

"Onward Captain."

Eddie stared at the forms on the island. He knew they could see them. They were standing there, watching, as they cruised away.

"They can see us. If they wanted to help us, all they would have to do is yell out."

"They'd probably use those guns on us, if we got too close."

"We'll never know."

Chuck followed the coastline of Staten Island. Staying close enough to feed his curiosity but far enough away to avoid any potential hazards.

In the cabin, Dawn and Alexis had decided to start bathing the kids. They took their dirty clothes and soaked them in the sink with shampoo, trying to wash them as best they could. There were plenty of t-shirts to go around and though large they were just fine for the kids to wear till they're clothes could be dried.

Alexis made them all brush their teeth. Not having many toothbrushes they all shared one. She hid this fact from them so they wouldn't complain about cooties or some such.

Frankie had made his way down and in the bright light of the cabin he could see how filthy he truly was. Especially when contrasted against the others, most of which had all showered and changed into new clothes.

When he stood in front of the mirror he noticed how large his beard had grown and how dark the circles around his eyes were. He noticed how dark his skin looked and couldn't tell whether it was from being dirty or from how much sun he'd been getting. And then he saw how much blood was on his hands and arms and clothes. It looked almost like he stuck his arms into large buckets of paint.

53 JUST ONE MORE DAY

Davis did in fact have a small arsenal stockpiled in his home, which was nearly secured as well as the Caulfield's.

"This is one hell of a collection, Sheriff."

"No more Sheriff, all right? Please."

"So, Bruce, how the hell did you get all these guns?"

"Some I've bought over the years, but most of these were recent acquisitions. Once martial law was declared. I cherry-picked some of these out of the armory, and some out of the confiscated arms we're supposed to turn over to the feds once a year. Feds are gonna have to wait," Davis said.

"I reckon they will," Walter nodded.

"Barbara make a decent shot?"

"Shoots a lot better than Jeff, that's for sure, probably better than me too, but she doesn't have to deal with arthritis."

"Well, grab whatever you think they can handle the best. I'm set with these," Davis said, hoisting up two police-issued shotguns.

"Hey Bruce, I think you had a good idea with walling off the town, but maybe it was too big too fast, ya know? Maybe if there's enough of us left in town we can start small. Start with a building, maybe a street…"

"Maybe. Right now, I'm going to start with the station. Honestly I just want to kill as many of those things as I can. I don't know if there's anyone left besides us so maybe we can talk about this later."

"Sure thing. I just wanted to think out loud."

"And Walter, thanks for going out scouting for folks. If there were more people like you and your family we might actually stand a chance of surviving this shit."

Davis locked up his house as Walter descended the stairs with several firearms slung over his shoulders. He handed both his kids a shotgun and handgun each, with ample ammunition for all. He kept an assault rifle for himself.

They drove back to the station and once they got closer the dead had scattered through the streets. Mostly they stayed together, almost like a pack, but some had splintered off. Others even went in the opposite direction.

Davis pulled over to one side, and Walter the other.

"Spread out and watch your fire. Slow and steady, okay?"

Walter nodded, stepping out of the truck and carrying his rifle at hip level, its weight felt good in his hands and reminded him of his younger years.

They walked down the street, spread out and one by one took down the deaders as they approached. The deaders moved slowly, some dragging broken limbs, other dragging their intestines along the street. Some moved with twisted ankles and limbs bent at unnatural angles.

The shotgun blasts roared like beasts and rifle fire cracked like thunder. The dead dropped to the ground, landing in writhing twitching messes. At closer range the shotguns reduced whole heads to red mist.

Soon the street, and the path to the station were covered in gore and blood.

Jones, Keith, and Clem had all been killed a second time, their bodies lay in the street like the others, twitching, trying to come back again.

"Come on, everybody in. It's clear."

"Damn, this place is a mess," Jeff said.

"It's not that bad. Just the path to the back is pretty nasty. Everything else is okay. Gonna have to board up those front doors though."

"So what now?" Walter asked.

"Now, we're done. It just hit me how exhausted and hungry I am. I'm going to go home, get some food and go to sleep."

"What about me?" Topher asked, sounding like hell and sweating bullets.

"I told you I'd take care of you, and I will."

"Bruce, why don't you all come back to our house? We got plenty of food, you can sleep there and we'll keep an eye on you. If we're all that's left of town, we should stick together."

"I'm too tired to argue. Danni, whattya say? Want to stick with us?"

"Yes. I have nowhere else to go. Thank you."

"Sure thing, kid. Bruce, maybe you want to swing back home, get some clean clothes. We'll follow you over."

"I can meet you there. Maybe just take--"

"No, not happening. Take your time do what you have to do and we'll wait outside for you. Then we'll follow you back and that's that."

"Thanks Walter."

Walter nodded and turned to Danni, "Danni was it? I'm Walter. These are my kids, Jeff, and Barbara."

"Hi..."

"Come on. Let's get out of here."

They left Davis and Topher in the station and stood in the carnage outside.

"How you feeling?"

"I feel like hell. You gonna do it now? You gonna kill me?"

"What do you want? Do you think you can make it a little longer?"

"I don't know. I feel like I'm on fire. This is awful, I tell ya."

"I'm sure it is. Topher, listen. I don't want to have to do this yet, so if you think you can hold out I think that'd be the best. Maybe a last meal or something? Maybe you want to down some pills and go out nice and quiet?"

"No, I want you to put a bullet in my brain. That's the only way isn't it?"

Davis knew different. He'd seen a good friend blow his brains out and come back for a taste of the living. But he knew Topher didn't need to know that. He just wanted to keep the man at ease and make it as quick and painless as he could. "Yeah, that's the only way to stay dead."

"Then that's how I want it. I don't want to come back."

"Okay. Let's get out of here, maybe take the edge off with a little Jack?"

"Yeah, that sounds good."

Topher started walking for the door.

"I'll be right behind ya, gonna grab a set of walkies."

Topher kept on walking. He opened the door, seeing the others walking over to the vehicles down the street. He turned to look down the other side of the street and could see the sun sagging low in the sky. It looked nice, there was a lot of blue, but some of the sunset colors were starting to come out. One more day, I can make it one more day. Just long enough to see another sunrise. I can do it...I can—

Davis blew his brains out of the front of his head, annihilating his last thought. Topher crumpled to the ground. Davis fired a few more times till all that was left of Topher's head resembled a rotting pomegranate.

54 FADING LIGHT

By now everyone but Chuck and Janice had showered. Janice didn't want to risk the safety of the others by doing so and no one argued with her. Even her sons didn't see the point. She was practically dead and could care less about how dirty she was.

Chuck just didn't want to have anyone else take the helm and potentially ruin what was becoming a pretty smooth trip.

Aside from the chill in the air, and eerily adrift vessels strewn about the Atlantic as if haphazardly thrown around by a child in a bathtub, it had been almost relaxing. They weren't running, being chased down by deaders, at the mercy of strangers, or travelling alongside a murderer.

The cigars had long ago been smoked to stubs and tossed overboard, but the scent still lingered. In Florida, Chuck spent a lot of time on boats. Almost always drinking. Sometimes fishing, sometimes partying, and sometimes doing other things. He loved the water. Felt at home on it. Loved the relaxing rhythms of its waves.

The soothing movements rocked everyone in the cabin to sleep except for Frankie. He was awake. In some yuppies clothes—clean clothes, however—and watching everyone else sleep. He was trying to come to terms with what his life was now. And tried to see ahead at what it could be. Aside from his best friend and his family, everything he loved was dead. It only recently began to sink in.

Maybe things would be different further up the coast. Maybe they would find a place in the world that still had a heartbeat.

Maybe there's something still ahead to live for...

Eventually his thoughts led to sleep and his body fell to the side, leaning against Abdul who fell asleep only moments before.

Topside, Eddie and Joseph sat with their mother, trying their best to comfort one another. While Scott and Judy sat bundled up with a fleece throw over their shoulders.

Chung-Hee hung around Scott, watching how he worked the ship and asking questions the whole while. It was clear to both of them what he was doing and why and Chuck was more than happy to answer his questions. He offered Chung-Hee the chance to pilot it for a while, but he declined.

"You keep doing it, I don't want to rock the boat."

"Don't worry about that. In a lot of ways the water is more forgiving than the roadways."

"Nah, it's okay, man. Maybe later. I think I'm going to go shower anyway."

"Suit yourself."

Once Chung-Hee stepped into the cabin he couldn't help but chuckle. Everyone was passed out and at least two people were snoring obscenely loudly. He found the light switch and dimmed it for them. He noticed everyone was wearing new clothes and he looked about the room trying to determine where they came from. He decided to look through what cabinets he could and found a pair of flannel pajama pants and a long sleeved thermal shirt.

"Good enough," he mumbled to himself and headed for the bathroom.

The night was clear and quiet. The moon shimmered on the water. Chuck stared into the distance and felt like he was staring into a void. Aside from the moon and the stars, there was nothing but darkness all around.

Judy fell asleep, her cheek pressed against Scott's chest. He pulled her close, making sure the fleece throw was wrapped tightly to her. He kept his eye on Chuck to make sure he wasn't falling asleep and kept his eyes on Janice to make sure she wasn't turning into one of the deaders.

His gaze fell on Eddie and Joseph. Two brothers who had been as tough as nails from the moment they met. Yet there they sat, distraught, broken, holding on to their mother as she slipped away into what Scott could only imagine as being a cold unforgiving darkness. Scott knew death—at least he thought he did—and the bodies he prepared for burial were always cold, as cold as ice sometimes, and devoid of any light. The eyes just didn't shine the same way in the light; even fingernails seemed to lose their sheen.

He could offer no words of solace. No sentiments to help ease the pain and lessen the grief. Maybe after all was said and done, but not now, all he could do now was witness it and stay alert.

Yussef slept uncomfortably. He shifted and spun, waking and falling back to sleep. He felt nauseous and was sweaty. He scratched at his lower leg, making bleed a small scratch he had no idea he'd gotten when Janice pulled him away from the deader on the bridge. Everyone else slept peacefully, undisturbed by his restlessness, but his restlessness only grew and so did the darkness inside him.

55 WISHFUL THINKING

At the Caulfield's, after Davis and Danni had cleaned up and put fresh clothes on, they sat down for dinner. It was clear that the two guests were famished as they barely spoke a word, scarfing down as much food as possible. When there was no more food left, Davis sat back and smiled.

"Mrs. Caulfield, that was superb."

"Thank you, Bruce. Anyone want coffee."

Everyone said, "Yes."

There was some small talk, some big talk, and many interruptions from the children. Aside from deaders, it was the first time Danni had seen living children since the first days. There was a dark situation when she took refuge with Clem and his wife, involving their granddaughter, but she couldn't blame them for keeping her.

She found the Caulfield children's smiles and laughter otherworldly. It was as if they had no concept of what was happening to the world in which they lived. She envied their ignorance, and their happiness even more so. Despite the loss of Clem, another tragic casualty in the day-to-day survival against the dead, she was happy to be here. Happy to be alive and surrounded by good people.

After awhile everyone dispersed, leaving Walter and Davis sitting at the table drinking coffee.

"I know I didn't want to get into it till I had some rest, but you got me thinking Walter."

"Thinking about what?"

"The wall...or walling off a smaller section at least. When we took down those deaders at the station I could see it right there. A small version of what I had in mind, something more practical I guess. We wouldn't even need much to do it because the buildings over there are so close together. We can probably get enough school busses to block off both ends of the street. Say from where the post office is, till the stop sign on the far end."

"And what about in between the buildings?"

"Well, some of them are so narrow we could literally wall 'em off if we can find enough materials. Or maybe just stick a car in there and fence it off, barricade it somehow. Some of the larger spaces I don't really know. Fencing, some trenches, regular patrols maybe?"

"Sure, any of that could work. I'm thinking though, that's a lot of work for just the few of us. Maybe tomorrow we'll go around and see if we can't round up some more people in town."

"Sounds fine to me. We'll just take it one step at a time."

"Amen to that. I just want to get the kids out for a bit tomorrow. They need to run around outside. Maybe you and the girl can help us keep an eye out. We've been trying to shelter them from the dead; it's starting to wear on us. We wanted to start working on fencing off the house and reinforce it anyway we could. We've been going around and scavenging supplies from the neighbors too."

"That's good man, thinking ahead. I should've started thinking ahead from day one. Maybe I could've made some better choices, kept more people alive..."

"Hindsight's always twenty-twenty. You reacted the way you should have. It's not like we were getting a lot of real information at first."

"No we weren't."

"You think this will pass?"

"I sure as shit hope so. Why wouldn't it? Maybe it'll go away as abruptly as it came. But I think that's just hopeful thinking. I think we'll be dealing with this for a long time to come."

"I was talking to Jeff the other day. About making it through the winter...it'll be tough on us, but maybe it'll be even tougher on the dead. Maybe if we can get some snow, some real bad weather, it'll help us out. They don't seem to take shelter, so if we get a bad winter..."

"More wishful thinking, Walt. I don't think we saw snow till

January last year."

"Then maybe we'll get it early this year."

"You got enough food to last that long?"

"No, not by a long shot, but we're getting there. There's a lot of homes in town and it's not like we have anything else to do."

"I guess not."

Jeff sat on the floor playing with the kids and Maria. Barbara stood by the door, looking outside. Laura sat with Danni, trying to engage her in conversation but she seemed to be drifting off into her own thoughts.

Barbara stepped outside, listening to the sounds of night settling in over the land. There was still enough light as the blue sky grew darker and darker to see her surroundings. She could see a few deaders bleeding into the darkness, getting lost into what would soon be night. It would be a clear night, she knew, as she looked up to the sky and saw a brilliant display of stars.

God, if you're listening…if you're even fucking out there, why? Why are you doing this? What the hell did we do?

56 VENGEANCE ON THE WIND

Sarah joined the dead horde that followed Ben through the house and down into the garage. He put the truck into reverse and drove it back off the ruined door. The dead now shambled over the door following after him. He pulled the truck over to a stop, got out and turned the latch on the back of the truck, with ease he pushed the door all the way up and pulled out the loading ramp.

"Get in you dead mother fuckers I ain't got all day!"

The dead did not argue. Though they did have a hell of a time trying to walk up the ramp. Some fell off, while others bumped into each other, some just didn't understand what it was they were supposed to be doing.

"Fucking idiots. Brain dead maggot sucking idiots."

Ben waited though; he wanted Sarah in the truck. Jim made it in, just barely, and Sarah wasn't far behind. Her movements were smoother than the others, more fluid, and less jerkily. She was a fresh one, and if Ben could figure out a way of getting hard, he wanted to fuck her—dead or not.

Eventually she got into the back of the box truck and Ben pulled down the door and locked the latch. He slammed the ramp back in and waived a middle finger to the deaders that were unable to load themself in.

Driving away, Creedence Clearwater Revival was still blasting from the speakers.

***

211

Ben drove on some sort of dark autopilot from hell. Driving casually through the mostly empty streets. Leaves littered the grounds and streets, clogged the storm drains, and kicked up into the air as Ben drove through them. He could tell which homes had people in them and which didn't. He knew the dead could as well, but they tended to get distracted and wander off.

Distraction was something Ben didn't care for too much. He liked to stay focused--to keep his eyes on the prize, as his father would say. So as much as he wanted to knock on the door and surprise a couple of survivors he drove on. Through the streets that would take him to New Haven and beyond. He would drive close to Titan City so he could see the beautiful destruction with his own decaying eyes.

Then he would get onto 287 and follow it as far north as he could because he knew that was the way to go.

How do I know?

Why do I know?

Are there others like me?

The darkness inside him answered without ever saying a word. Feeling elated Ben drove on. The dead moved out of his way when he approached, in the few spots where they moved like sheep across the highway. It made him feel like some kind of zombie royalty, a dead knight in putrefying armor.

He was part of something now. Something far bigger than he ever thought possible—The Unwinding.

He loved killing, and had aspired to be listed among the greats. He always hoped he'd get a movie made of his dark art once it was all said and done, but now? The greats were small fish. He was swimming in a sea of blood that would drown the world, and in it he was a shark.

Just like those he followed he had to abandon his vehicle. He let the dead out of the back of the truck and walked away. Dead Sarah and the others followed behind, shuffling noisily through a pile of cans on the side of the road.

Ben walked quickly, with a determination in his stride unhindered like the others behind him whose dead bones and flesh weakened and withered into a slow almost unending decay.

If he had breath, it would probably be visible with the chill in the air, but nothing came out of his lungs. His chest didn't move, his thickening blood only pumped as a result of his movements and he could feel it. It felt like thick oil barely able to move through his veins, being pushed up from his toes like sludge only to slide back down.

He made it to the bridge. His dead friends far behind, but other deaders in his vicinity had come to be near him, drawn to him like some sort of death magnet.

By the time he made it to the top of the bridge he knew he was too late. He could hear the boat approaching. He rushed to the side to watch as the living vermin escaped his wrath once again. Like rats on the water they scurried away.

Fucking pussies. Run. I'll get ya. I'll find ya and I'll tear yer God damned hearts out.

Then he felt it. He could feel the death in their group. One or more of them were dying. The darkness inside them was growing.

Or maybe I won't have to…

…maybe you'll all be dead before I can get to ya.

EPILOGUE

West Virginia.
Mount Weather Special Facility.

As commanded, Rachel and Tran reported to The Deputy Secretary of Defense's makeshift office. The room was dusty and smelled like an old library. He sat behind a dark, large desk that took up half the room. It made him look small, but no less fierce. His face was stuck in a perpetually angry grimace. Even his hands looked angry. They were dry with large knuckles that undoubtedly had met many faces in his younger years.

"Sit," he paused for a moment, then continued, "let's get right to it. I've already dispatched a unit of my men to a nearby prison."

"West Virginia Penitentiary?"

"Yes, now don't interrupt me till I finish."

"Sorry sir--"

"What did I just say? If the prison is operational, with real live prisoners, my men will be securing the facilities. If not, then it's back to the drawing board. Since I'm an optimist we'll assume the facilities can be secured in a matter of days. They will then establish a mode of transportation to make regular trips so that you have a supply of fresh bodies. In the event that should prove difficult we'll move the two of you and whatever supplies and equipment you need over there."

"What? You can't be serious."

"Of course I'm serious. Now sit. The fuck. Down. If that happens, you'll have a small unit with you at all times. I don't want the two of you getting killed, but I think what the two of you are doing is important. Now I'm not sold on what you're selling me, but we've got to follow it through. We all want to be somewhere else. We all want this shit to be over with, but it isn't going to happen unless we make it happen. Understood?"

"Yes, sir."

"Understood, sir."

"You two can go rest up or do whatever it is you white-coats do around here. I expect to hear from the team within the hour and I'll update you both as soon as possible."

Tran stood up first and made his way out of the room as quickly as possible. He wasn't a fan of the Secretary, or of men like him, and saw no reason to stay in his company any longer.

"Slow down," Rachel called.

"Sorry, I just want to get away from the jerk."

"He wasn't so bad. I get the feeling he's just putting up a tough front."

"I doubt it. I don't think there's much more to that man other than what we see."

"Don't rush to judgment."

"Never, but sometimes a brick wall is a brick wall."

"Okay. Well, see you in a bit. I'm going to catch a catnap."

"If you can't sleep, I'll be having tea, and you're welcome to join me."

"Thank you."

Tran nodded and turned down the corridor toward his quarters. Rachel continued forward, en route to her own room.

Once there she kicked off her shoes and threw herself back into her unmade bed. She pulled the covers around herself and wrapped them tightly around her shoulders and she nuzzled her face into a pillow.

She wanted to think of nothing. To just close her eyes and sleep a dreamless sleep. But when she closed her eyes all she could think about was how the hell she ended up in this nightmare life inside a mountain.

Why her and not someone else? She remembered how the Federal

Agent and two fatigued men came to her door. If she'd said "No," instead of "Yes," they would have grabbed her and taken her away all the same. She knew that for a fact as some of her colleagues had said "No," yet they were here all the same.

The day they arrived here the Secretary addressed them all in a large group in the dining area. She remembered how he made it sound like it was their duty to figure out what was happening and why, and most importantly, how to stop it.

She could hear Pymn's voice still echoing in the large room, "You are all that stands in the way of our demise. Some of you may be wondering why you're even here. What could you possibly have to offer? Well, you are all we could find on short notice and in relative vicinity. There are several other outposts such as ours with similar teams assembled. Unfortunately we have lost contact with all of them. We simply do not know if they were successful in getting their teams together and sequestered away. There is much we do not know. It is your job to find out more."

Then her mind jumped forward to yesterday and all she could think about was death. When she was a young teen, the Grim Reaper was cool. Death was a skeleton with bloodshot eyes, a tattered purple hood, and a gleaming scythe. Rock bands and Heavy Metal bands sang songs about him.

She remembered how her lungs felt like ice, how her hands were almost frozen, even waning in pallor. The entire room seemed to drop in temperature as the dead soldier spoke. And then she thought of him. The dead soldier, the man who looked like a scared boy. She thought of how easily they exchanged his life for a few words. They had no right to do that. She had no right.

Maybe that's why Death has come…because we don't have any respect for life…

END

ABOUT THE AUTHOR

Steve Wands lives in New Jersey with his wife and son. He's a freelance artist by day and writer by night. He drinks too much coffee, and sleeps very little. He is the author of the *Stay Dead* series of short stories, collections, and novels as well as *Horror Stories: A Macabre Collection, Words Like Daggers, Modern Nightmares,* and plenty of short stories. He also co-edited and contributed to *Dark: A Horror Anthology.*

You can visit his blog here: http://www.stevewands.blogspot.com or play with his twitter: http://twitter.com/swands

If Google Groups are your thing, then why not join Steve's: http://groups.google.com/group/apparatus-revolution

www.ingramcontent.com/pod-product-compliance
Lightning Source LLC
Chambersburg PA
CBHW022014170626
46808CB00001B/400